LAST GATE
OF
THE EMPEROR

LAST GATE
OF THE EMPEROR

KWAME MBALIA
PRINCE JOEL MAKONNEN

THORNDIKE PRESS
A part of Gale, a Cengage Company

GALE

Thorndike Press® Large Print Striving Reader Collection.
The text of this Large Print edition is unabridged.
Other aspects of the book may vary from the original edition.
Set in 16 pt. Plantin.

LIBRARY OF CONGRESS CIP DATA ON FILE.
CATALOGUING IN PUBLICATION FOR THIS BOOK
IS AVAILABLE FROM THE LIBRARY OF CONGRESS.

ISBN-13: 978-1-4328-9158-9 (hardcover alk. paper)

Published in 2021 by arrangement with Scholastic Inc.

Printed in Mexico
Print Number: 01   Print Year: 2022

To the Black children of the Diaspora, who have always been the future.
— Kwame Mbalia

To Ariana, Adey, Yokshan, Leah, and Ephrem. And all the children of Ethiopia; you stand on the shoulders of her rich past, with her bright future in your eyes.
— Prince Joel Makonnen

Audio Transcript File No. 2132.019

Location: [UNDISCLOSED DE-TENTION FACILITY]

Time: 00:45

Subject: Yared [LAST NAME RE-DACTED FOR SECURITY]

Auditor: Now, then. Start from the beginning. Again. For the third time. State your name for the audio file.

Me: Yared.

Auditor: *Full* name.

Me: Yared [REDACTED].

Auditor: . . .

Me: Listen, I didn't name myself. If I did, my last name would be 'TheGr8.' One word. And a number.

Auditor: . . .

Me: I even tried to change my name at school. They wouldn't let me. Ask them.

Auditor: We have. Speaking of, we pulled your school records and —

Me: Perfect, right? Stellar student, incredibly smart with tons of potential.

Auditor: — you barely attend class.

Me: . . .

Auditor: . . .

Me: Whaaaaat? No way. I go to class! All the time! Right there, at . . . at . . .

Auditor: Addis Prime Primary.

Me: Exactly. Addis Prime Primary. Good old . . . AP Squared. That's what we call it for short. AP Squared.

Auditor: Enough of these games, boy! You *will* start telling us everything you know.

Me: Oh, that's easy; I've got top marks in the class. My history teacher said my presentation was absolutely incredible. In fact, if not for the weird creature that nearly destroyed half the city, my presentation would have been the most exciting thing to happen all day.

Auditor: *Finally.* Let's talk about that.

Me: My presentation? Gladly!

Auditor: No, the mon—

Me: It started like this . . .

CHAPTER ONE

Once there was an empire that stretched across the galaxy. Great. Noble. Wardens of peace and good fortune, they spread wealth and technology throughout the stars. This empire was called Axum.

When Axumite ships landed in a new star system and made contact with the residents, they offered to teach them, to bring them into the Empire, sharing their knowledge and power. That was how their empire continued to grow. All sentient races and species were invited, and though some did refuse, many accepted.

But of those that accepted entry into the Empire, there was one that grew jealous. These people coveted Axum's technology, for they came from a barren planet whose resources had been exhausted, and they longed to take to the stars to find new riches to exploit. But they didn't want to share . . . they wanted to rule.

They were called the Werari.

The Werari bided their time, waiting until Axum was distracted with the Emperor and Empress's new baby . . . and then they struck. Using stolen Axumite technology, they conquered one peaceful planet after another. Planets. Space stations. Asteroid colonies. The Werari enslaved them all, then continued across the galaxy like unstoppable conquerors. And to help, they unleashed a terrible monster, a creature of such hatred and violence that none could stand in its way.

Its name was the Bulgu.

But the Emperor and Empress of Axum fought back. Their bodyguards were the legendary Meshenitai, unparalleled warriors who wielded curved shotels wreathed in black flame. The Meshenitai were fierce. They fought like demons, with incredible speed and power. The Axumite army, the Living Flames of the Burning Legion, defended their nation until the bitter end.

And it *was* a bitter end.

Just when it looked like Axum would prevail, a traitor — someone known and loved by the royal family — robbed them of their source of strength: the power that let the mighty nation travel between the stars. Axum was trapped, and they and the Werari fell into a war of attrition. It was a stalemate. The battle stretched over months, then years, with no one really winning but no clear loser. It is said that even today the Emperor and Empress still fight, together with their Meshenitai. They stand firm beneath the onslaught of the Bulgu. But without their source of strength, neither they nor the Werari could travel through space, and the two warring nations fell into darkness and out of history.

"And that's what shooting stars are," I said, looking out over the integrated virtual classroom. "Whenever you see one in the night sky, it's the Meshenitai and the Werari still battling high above our heads, granting you the power to reach for the sky . . ."

"Thank you, Yared," came a voice from

the corner.

"Which is why . . ." I continued, "I am asking for the Authority Net flight restrictions to be discontinued. How can we reach for the sky if our hands get zapped? Everyone deserves flying rights above the ridiculous ten-meter limit. There are hundreds of drones just waiting to harass kids like me — it's despicable."

"Yared," Mrs. Marjani warned.

"Seriously, who do they think they are? How are we supposed to make it to school on time if the streets are clogged in the mornings and a dutiful student can't fly a skysail over them? Does the Authority hate school?"

The lights in the class came on, and I blinked twice. Mrs. Marjani, one of my favorite teachers, actually, frowned at me as she walked to the front of the class. Even though it looked crowded, only twelve of the seventy-five students attending the lecture were physically present. It was the strangest thing, and I'd only been at Addis Prime Primary for a month, so it took some getting used to.

Well, let me take that back. The school itself was cool. Addis Prime Primary had been converted from an old factory overlooking a giant lake just inside New Oromia, the largest city on the space colony Addis Prime. Massive conveyor belts ran through huge vaulted tunnels underground to the shopping district, and utility drones buzzed in and out throughout the day, picking up supplies for the school. Do you know what that means? That means *if* someone was so inclined, they could hitch a ride on a floating metal bug the size of a cow, and take it all the way to the largest collection of goods and delicacies this side of the galaxy.

If they were so inclined.

I would never do that, not during school hours. Even if the most important game tournament in my life was taking place *in that shopping district* in less than an hour. No, that would be irresponsible. Rules, you know?

At my old school on the other side of the colony, every student had to attend, no matter how far away they lived. Here, the majority of the students were virtual. They were represented by drones or, if their families could afford it, holographic displays. Sometimes even the teachers were virtual. Unfortunately, not Mrs. Marjani. She marched silently forward, passing through two small, beetle-like drones — Haji and Kofi — that were wrestling in midair. She ignored them and stopped in front of me.

"Absolutely incredible," she said. Mrs. Marjani was a tall, short-haired woman from the highlands of Tigray Central. The light of the holoprojector with my presentation tinted her dark skin blue, giving her a magical aura. She was the most popular teacher at Addis Prime Primary. She was also the strictest.

"Thank you!" I said, smiling.

"It is absolutely incredible that you decided to give a presentation with no historical basis or relevancy. I mean, honestly, Yared. Did you even do the research? I asked you to present on the regional differences between New Oromia and Tigray Central, and you had a whole month! Instead you come back with . . . with fairy tales?"

"This is history! And I worked so hard on it. I sat with my uncle Moti every night for a week, pulling that story out of him. Do you know how many sambusas I had to fry? How many cups of tej I had to pour for him? My fingers are going to smell like oil and honey for a month."

The class snickered. Mrs. Marjani pointed at my workstation. "Sit," she said, squeezing the single word through gritted teeth.

As I walked back to my seat, Haji's drone buzzed over and sat on my shoulder. "Way to go, Yared," came a tiny voice. The drone's speaker was barely audible. "She looks like she's ready to explode. I thought you said you were going to give a presentation so good she'd let you go home early. The game starts in forty-five minutes. If you're late, the admins will —"

I flicked the drone aside. He didn't need to tell me how important the upcoming game was. His number-one ranking wasn't on the line. "I know, I know. Trust me, I've got this. Any second now."

Mrs. Marjani was still lecturing me from the front of the class. "And if you applied an ounce of effort to your studies, instead of your ridiculous exploits, you might actually pass this class and others."

"But the story —" I began to say.

"Is not true," Mrs. Marjani snapped. Was it just me or did she look angrier than I'd ever seen her? And . . . nervous? But I couldn't linger on that too long; she was still lecturing me. "And I am not putting up with your shenanigans today. Report to independent study. I expect a full *revised* presentation on the history of Addis Prime by tomorrow morning. Dismissed. The rest of you, screens out. Please load the holovid labeled 2109-A."

Everyone groaned. A few people shot angry glares my way. I didn't meet their eyes. This was my fourth school in two years, and it looked like I'd spend my time here like I did at all the others.

Alone.

Independent study was in a large room in the center of the school equipped with study pods so students could focus on exams or final projects. It was silent as a crypt, and the only door was monitored by securi-drones that would set off an alarm if they caught you trying to sneak out.

However, the study hall *also* happened

to be right next to one of the underground conveyor tunnels. With multiple windows overlooking the entrance. I hid a smile as I gathered up my things. I may not have made many friends yet, but I *was* closer to fame and glory. This afternoon, when everyone found out who I really was? My name would be written in the stars.

I winked at Haji's drone and walked out of class. I loved this school.

I hated this school.

"Why did they have to serve yasa tibs for lunch?" I said with a groan.

There I was, clinging to a tiny ledge two stories off the ground, a skinny brown boy two inches from toppling into a garbage chute, trying to plot how I was going to avoid falling into fish bones and spicy sauce to achieve my plan.

It was the middle of the day. I was hot and sweaty, and my partner in crime was being a giant baby. Although the securidrones hadn't spotted me slipping out the window, the cleaning bots were on a roll.

Literally.

Their massive magnetized brushes swept dirt and attracted scraps, and if they caught me outside the classroom, the four-armed robotic custodians with massive wheels instead of legs would start their chase, brushes spinning, ready to grab me like a crumpled piece of trash and carry me off to the headmistress's office to earn a bunch of demerits. Part humanoids, part cars, 100 percent snitches. Nothing good would come from being spotted. The school would call my uncle Moti (again) and I'd get a stern lecture (also again) filled with several long sighs and a couple of head shakes, and . . . Look, no one wants that. Even now, three bots patrolled the hallway just inside the window.

Luckily, they hadn't seen me yet.

Unfortunately, they had detached their brushes and were carrying large trash cans filled with lunchtime leftovers, ready to deposit them through the chute your intrepid hero (me) currently hid in, where it would flow down and into one of the city's many automated hovercans. I'd tried to gunk up their gears by tossing a few styluses at their wheels when they weren't looking (speaking of which, I was going to have to borrow a stylus when I came back), and it slowed them for a bit, but now they all clustered together. Sneaking back into the study hall at this point would be risky. Dangerous, even. Especially when the hovercan was way behind schedule.

I looked down and groaned. Where was that silly thing?

I only had thirty minutes left to register and get to the site for the game. The Hunt for Kaleb's Obelisk — or the HKO, as we all called it — was a massive augmented reality tournament. And though it was the best game to ever exist, the people who ran it, the game admins, were sticklers about punctuality. That was because the game was played in public. The locations rotated, and you only got a code if you were in a specific spot at a specific time. If you didn't make it, sorry, better luck next time. Any and all points you'd earned were wiped and you were dropped to the bottom of the rankings. And since the top-two ranked players could rake in a fortune in prize money, there was no way I was going to be late.

I looked below, trying to find my hovercan ride in all the chaos. Addis Prime spread out around me in a carpet of muddled brown and dingy gray. The school stood on a hill, so I could see each of the woredas, the districts of Addis Prime, and the traffic flowing in and out of them. Hovertrucks piled high with mangos and all kinds of chilis and papayas headed to the Gebeya to be sold in market stalls. Floating rickshaws honked their way through, carrying important, well-dressed people into Authority Central at the very middle. Night-shift workers shuffled onto crowded buses to head home. Simple drones floated in front of each of the oval transports, flashing the route and kebele the bus would take. Loud coffee vendors, in their fluttering pedal carts, boasted about the strength of their beans and waved steaming jebenas in the air, ready to pour the perfect cup.

I clung to my handholds on the tiny ledge, trying to see if the blue of the sky would finally peek through the clouds. But all I saw was the occasional spark of the Net that supposedly kept us safe.

Right. Safe.

Anyway.

The Authority Net floated high in the sky. Technically, it was a giant swarm of insect-like drones, all linked to one another and hearing the same instructions from the giant transmitter outside the entrance to New Oromia, where the Authority was headquartered. Each drone was the size of my arm, and bristling with stun turrets that fired immobilizing electric beads. One hit from those and you were frozen in an electric stasis field until someone came to release you. And believe me, they take their sweet time.

Remind me to tell you about that sometime.

The drones bobbed up and down and leaked metallic smoke that billowed above Addis Prime, so we rarely saw the sky. It also really, *really* messed with reception.

One day when I was bored (I'm always bored), I scrolled through my school-issued tablet and found an old picture of a large, nearly transparent creature that apparently lived in the ocean. It was named a jellyfish. Strange. Sometimes they would travel in groups and the water currents would make them float away. That's what the Net reminded me of, except instead of being carried off, they lingered overhead, keeping an eye on us for the Authority . . . and blocking everything else out, like the worst filter ever.

The Authority ruled Addis Prime, stiff and stern and no-nonsense. As far as I could tell, they were all adults in gray-and-white uniforms. They made up new rules constantly and tried to catch you breaking them, because disobedience was big business. More fines, more birr to pay. No running through the streets. No shouting or playing or backflips in public. And worst of all, no unauthorized flying. If you were caught entering the no-fly zone, ten meters above the ground, without the correct papers, *zap!* The drones would hit you with a stasis field, and they'd haul your frozen butt off to face serious consequences. So no flying.

No flying? Really?

I mean, really . . . what kind of stupid rule is that? Yeah, you could get permits, but those cost money. Surprise! Who would've guessed? Everyone who could afford the authorization had sails these days. Skysails, moonsails, even sunsails. If you didn't have one of the newest models of the powered glider, you just weren't cool. But, no birr in Yared's account (okay, Uncle Moti's account) meant no skysail, no authorization, and no hope.

Unless I got creative. Besides, piloting a skysail out of the school's window to the HKO would have definitely drawn too much attention. However, no one said anything about falling slowly into an unsuspecting ride.

Yared, one; the system designed to keep him down, zero.

The only problem was that when I came up with this plan to skip school by jumping in a robo-driven trash can, I was supposed to have my nefasi with me. I'd built the special backpack with leftover thrusters and antigrav padding from Uncle Moti's workshop. Nothing like being able to carry your school supplies *and* hang out a few meters in the air.

But last night, the power to the factory

we'd converted into a home cut off again, and the engineers hadn't started repairs yet. Without a charge, the nefasi was useless, so I'd left it behind. All of this was annoying, but the worst part was Uncle Moti. He hadn't even complained. He just sighed and got dressed for work. Uncle Moti liked to stay on the right side of the law and not cause any fuss. It got on my nerves. Sometimes you had to shake things up a bit!

That nefasi would've been useful because I modified it to hold extra weight. The extra weight currently clinging to my shoulders. With her claws. Remember the partner in crime I mentioned earlier? I was referring to my big diranium scaredy-cat, Besa. Yes, my best friend also happened to be a bionic cat. Technically, she was a lioness. She always tried to follow me everywhere, but you try hiding a giant feline while running an errand to pick up Sleep-Tree leaves for your uncle. She came up to my knees and her metallic skin gleamed bright silver. I normally kept her at home during the day. Unfortunately, she was my secret weapon for the HKO. And, just my luck, she was afraid of heights.

"Mrowr?"

"No," I lied through gritted teeth. "You're fine. Not heavy at all."

I could make this jump, no problem. I'd done it plenty of times before. But with a bionic mouse-hunter draped all over me? Yeesh, this was going to be a jump for the ages. Maybe I should've just tossed my hairless feline friend when I first hopped out the window.

"Mrrrrow?" she whimpered.

"No, Besa, nooooo. Why would you say that? I would never toss you. We're family!"

"Mrrow."

"No, look. We're going to jump together. Promise. I'm just waiting for the perfect time."

You'd think something with nine lives and a diranium shell would take more risks.

"Mrrow."

"Yeah, well, next time you can come up with the plan."

Just then, a door slammed from inside

the window. I pressed myself flat against the trash chute. Just what I needed. Witnesses.

"What are these cleaning bots doing all clumped up in the study hall? Most of them are still empty. Mrs. Marjani, please notify the manufacturer that they're malfunctioning again."

I froze. That was the headmistress's voice. What was she doing here? *And* Mrs. Marjani! No, no, no — this was going to ruin everything.

A low boom sounded in the distance. The vibrations shook the tiny ledge. Besa dug her claws into my shoulder, and I winced. I strained, trying to listen in on the conversation slipping out the open window.

"Of course, Headmistress," Mrs. Marjani replied.

Wait.

There was no problem. The adults just didn't realize the silly machines were doing their jobs trying to capture me — to glue me to their brushes like a piece of soggy injera and turn me in. Metallic traitors.

A low humming sound filled the air. I closed my eyes in relief. Finally. The hovercan rounded the corner, its antigrav thrusters growing louder. Almost time. I tensed, getting ready to make my escape while the headmistress sighed loudly.

"So our favorite new student isn't doing too well?"

"I'm giving him space to adjust," Mrs. Marjani said slowly. "But the stories he tells in class, the ones he relays from his uncle . . ."

"Yes, the ones from your report. Hmm. The uncle is the guardian, correct? I received a note from him requesting another meeting. He wants to discuss next year's enrollment fees. I was planning on sending him the standard reply, but I wanted to wait for a report on the boy's progress. It seems he might not be cut out for this."

"Perhaps if I could work with him one-on-one —"

"No, we discussed this. We don't have the resources for that. Your class size is large enough as it is. No, I'll send the response. School policy, prompt payments to be expected, and so on and so forth. If I have to read one more message begging for more time to pay . . ." The headmistress cleared her throat, probably realizing she was complaining. "Yes, well. Thank you for this latest report, Mrs. Marjani."

Uncle Moti was . . . begging? For me?

My head drooped as anger and embarrassment filled my chest.

"Yes, Headmistress," Mrs. Marjani replied, her voice resigned. I felt as if I'd let her down. Maybe I should've worked a bit harder on that presentation. When I got back from the tournament, I would redouble my efforts.

"That kid is really too much trouble," the headmistress's voice said, growing fainter. "Always breaking the rules. So many unpaid fines. What is his uncle thinking? Next year's enrollment will be conditional on the payment of all outstanding fees and tuition, *plus* next year's tuition up front."

Hot tears pricked at the corners of my eyes, threatening to roll down my cheek. I shook my head angrily. Stupid school.

Antigrav brakes squealed down the

street. I lifted my head and wiped away the tears.

Stupid expensive school, with its tiny ledges and short independent study period. A timer went off on my wrist comm. Twenty minutes to get registered for this week's tournament. A fierce grin crept across my face. One last time. I would play HKO one last time, win, and cash out my ranking for a hovercan full of birr. When I returned this afternoon, just before the final period, it would be to dump a pile of money on the head-mistress's desk. Uncle Moti would never have to stoop to begging for anything again.

The hovercan rumbled closer. The floating garbage truck was driverless, its route preprogrammed. Every day, just after noon, it floated beneath the school and collected the lunchtime trash that those awful cleaning bots discarded via the chute. Today, it was my ride out of here.

I steadied myself.

Stupid school.

Stupid power outages.

Stupid rules.

They were all useless. Uncle Moti always said rules were guides to a prosperous future, but I had a different saying: What's a rule if not an invitation to break it? I just had to find a way to get around it. That's just what I was going to do. I had a date with the game of the century, and I wasn't going to miss it for anything. I'd get that money. I'd be famous. They wouldn't be able to talk about me like that again. Or Uncle Moti. They'd beg me to stay and keep spending our money there. They'd print my face on their electronic brochure.

The hovercan flew right under me. I tensed as the cleaning bots started beeping again, a warning no one else heard. My heart thudded in my chest. My eyes grew wide.

"Time to go!"

"Mrowr!"

"Sorry, Besa, we have to jump . . . now!"

I hurled myself through the air, loving the feel of the wind through my curls, freedom filling my soul, as if this was the only thing I was meant to do.

Soar, Yared. Soar.

CHAPTER TWO

I was flying. Really flying! Well, without my nefasi, maybe it was just falling dramatically. Flying sounded a lot better than falling dramatically, though. Makes the whole thing sound more impactful in a story.

Speaking of impactful . . .

I landed inside the hovercan, crashing into a pile of moldy banana peels, coffee-ground sludge, and used rags. Used for what, I couldn't tell. And then, as if this adventure hadn't already gotten off to an amazing start . . .

Splat.

Wet, fishy leftovers from the yasa tibs splashed onto my clothes. The garbage chute had emptied its guts all over me. I looked up to see the cleaning bots beeping away in the window above. They'd probably be laughing, if humor could be programmed. I sat up and scooted away from the pile of absolutely *fantastic* smells, leaning against the metal wall of the hovercan as it continued to its next stop at the building next door.

Something rattled under my shirt, and I pulled out an all-black hexagon medallion, silver wire braided around the edges, a lion roaring in the middle. I kissed it, grimaced at the bit of trash on it, then tucked it beneath my shirt again. Uncle Moti had given it to me several years back, and it had come to represent the two of us. Defiant to the end. Life had dealt us some blows, but we never let that stop us.

"Well," I said after a deep breath. "We made it, Besa. Start the countdown. If we're not back in two hours, it won't matter if Uncle Moti can pay the tuition or not — because he'll ground me for the rest of my life."

Next to me, a boxy snout made of once-polished diranium and used-to-be-sleek carbon fiber emerged from beneath a large fish bone. The battered silver-and-black lioness quirked her ears at me rudely.

"Yeah, yeah," I said. "Laugh it up. He doesn't give *you* the 'we have to be leaders' speech." And it was true. Uncle Moti could be strict. Best behavior, act like someone's always watching. (*Because, more than likely, someone is watching,* he'd say.) And excel at whatever you attempt. He was always giving me additional homework, and sometimes he'd set exercises for me. Strategy sessions. Tactics. Even archery lessons. Yes, war-bows and arrows.

Sometimes I think he knew about me and the HKO, and this was his way of unofficially helping me. Why else have me work on pincer formations, terrain advantages, and other stuff like that? Then again, adults were weird, so who knew?

The hovercan slogged through the tunnel, emerging in an alley between a comm tower and a store advertising light-adaptive holographic displays called screens. They could project images above them that ranged in size from a button to giant billboard-sized placards, like the one in the auditorium at school. In fact, we had a lot of screens in the school. Each student at Addis Prime Primary got one . . . Well, those who paid the fee.

Yeah, guess who that didn't include?

The hovercan hummed along to the Gebeya to get even more trash from the midday market shoppers. And, lucky for me, to unknowingly drop me at the registration site. The game changed locations every year so the Authority couldn't catch on.

A chime alerted me. I checked my wrist comm — time to log in. "All right, Besa. Let me check your diagnostics." A virtual keyboard appeared next to her shoulder. Uncle Moti had helped me program her, and despite her dents and dings, she was state-of-the-art. So what if there were a few scratches here or there (on me, not on her — her claws are sharp)? Ever my trusty companion, she was also a computer capable of hooking into the Nexus, the communications network that linked all of Addis Prime.

I scanned her systems and made sure everything was good to go — I didn't want to go into the game with Besa at less than full strength. Power levels were steady, targeting looked great, and her hidden snack cubby was loaded. Never knew when the munchies would strike. Finally, I checked her firmware and made sure everything was up to date. Couldn't be too careful.

"All good here," I said happily.

"Mrowr."

"Of course I didn't expect anything different. Better to be safe, right?"

"Mrowr."

"Wow, you're cocky. Let's just log in." Besa sat on her metal haunches at my side, her mouth open in something midway between a yawn and a roar. A cone of light hit the opposite wall of the hover-can, turning it into a makeshift screen. A giant but familiar face was projected in front of me, looking slightly worried.

Haji.

" 'TheGr8' is ready to enter HKO. Slide me the location, Haji."

My classmate and one of the in-game moderators squinted at something, then winced. "Sorry, Yared, I don't see that name on here."

"Wait, what do you mean?" I said. "Check again!"

"I did. You're not here. Did you register?"

I pounded my fist into the floor. "I don't have to! I've won the last two out of four matches. I should've been automatically entered! I'm just here for the location."

"I know, I know, but the admins purged the database. That's why I told you to get here early. Everyone has to start at level one. Something about a new update. There's still time for you to get in; you just have to register as a new user. And . . . well, there's a new catch."

My heart fell into my slightly damp, definitely dirty boots. "What do you mean?"

"You have to register with your own name. Something about preventing fraud."

Alarm bells rang in my head. Uncle Moti was always wary of me putting my information on the Nexus. He would spend hours talking about security and people taking my identity. If I registered for HKO with my real name, there's no telling what sort of trouble we could get into. I mean, I wasn't a fool. We'd been moving around for as long as I could remember, and he was extremely careful to make sure we didn't get into trouble.

Once, when I came home from my old school with a holovid yearbook, my name floating below a younger, snaggle-toothed Yared, Uncle Moti nearly had a heart attack. Packed up everything and moved us out that night. Just because I wanted to take a class picture. Strange, right? Nothing even happened.

I sighed. "Come on, Haji. Don't do me like this. I got through all the prelim levels with no problems. And that was a whole lot of birr tied up on that old account. Can't I reactivate it?"

Haji shook his head. The slightly chubby, brown-skinned boy was from the Historic Oromo region. He wore his hair in the new trend, curly and swept over his eyes, the sides of his head shaved into striking geometric designs. He spoke with a soft voice in his native tongue, and my Orominya was a bit rusty, so I had to lean in close to Besa's speaker to hear. "Sorry,

Yared. Can't do it. That purge caught us all by surprise yesterday. Didn't have time to throw up shields, and all the servers got reset. We're lucky we can run it at all. So you'll have to start from zero. Now, look, I don't have time for this. The first round is about to start. Do you want in or not?"

I bit my bottom lip, my thoughts racing. After all this trouble, I couldn't just turn around and go back to school. No way. I had to make this work. It was too huge! Even if I didn't start at the top of the leaderboard, the prize money would set me and Uncle Moti up for the rest of our lives. Money couldn't buy everything, but it *would* solve a lot of problems. That's what Uncle Moti always said when he had to find a powerstream technician to get the lights working in our home. Money would help us move into a better place and get me a real bed instead of a dusty, beat-up smart-couch that tried to eat me if I slept on it wrong. Money would allow Uncle Moti to finally go to an Authority-approved doctor and see about the cough that left him hacking on the floor sometimes.

But I also wanted the glory. I was tired of being the new kid, the troublemaker, the failure. If I did this, I'd have everyone's respect. That's what I really wanted. To soar so high that everyone would see me, and everyone who logged in to the Nexus would know my name.

Yared, the kid from Addis Prime.

Yared, the kid who was the champion of HKO.

Yared, the kid you wanted to be best friends with.

And the glory . . .

The glory.

"Fine," I told Haji. "Yes, I want to play, no matter what."

"Good." He hesitated, then continued. "Well then, the battle royale starts in a few minutes, and everyone's at level one. No automatic skipping to upper levels. No prelim guarantees. But you have to register with your real name; that's the rule. If they catch you and something's out of order, you *and* me will be in trouble. Besides, you can customize your display name once you get in the game."

"Maybe if —"

"No maybes; I told the same thing to the Ibis."

That name stopped my begging cold. My jaw clenched, and a growl rumbled somewhere deep in Besa's chest. The Ibis was one of the top-ranked competitors, too. My rival, really. Remember I said I won the last two out of four HKOs? The Ibis had won the other two. And if the Ibis had to start in the opening round, there really wasn't any other option for me. Champion's privilege was out the window. I'd have to start from the bottom, too.

"Fine."

That didn't change anything. I had a secret advantage, and she was sitting right next to me, swishing her metallic jointed tail so that bits of trash flew into my face.

Ugh.

"That's my boy," Haji said, his image rippling on the rusted wall of the hovercan. "Sending over the coordinates now."

A series of numbers flashed below the display, and the first prickle of apprehension appeared. "The Gebeya? It's going to be crowded this time of day." The Gebeya was the main market in Addis Prime, and . . . well, it was huge. Beyond huge. But even more important, it would be swarming with Authority guards. And, well . . . the Authority didn't take too kindly to HKO players. In fact, getting caught competing in the tournament got you in as much trouble as being caught flying. Those folks just didn't like fun.

"That's what the admins chose. Be sure to authenticate as soon as you get here. I'll be waiting. And be careful, the streets beneath the Gebeya will be chaotic." Haji raised an eyebrow and opened his mouth as if he wanted to add something else, but at that moment, the hovercan began to slow to its final stop.

"Be there in a minute," I said. "Don't worry about me. This is my day. Stick around, I might let you smell my winnings."

Haji rolled his eyes.

I nodded at Besa, and she shut her jaws, effectively cutting the connection just as a strange expression crossed the boy's face. Concern? Fear? I ignored it, though, and prepared to slip out of my spotted me climbing out of a hovercan in the middle of the day, they could make a few birr by alerting the Authority securidrones. Snitches got paid well in Addis Prime.

"Selam, friend!" a robotic voice blared from behind me.

I whipped around. Besa growled and dropped into a low crouch, a sure sign she was about to pounce.

Bobbing in midair in front of us was a spinning pyramid the size of my head. Bright silver with horizontal gold lines, the object glimmered like a star that had fallen to earth. It was beautiful. Splendid. An absolute treasure.

I hated these things.

I rolled my eyes and threw a slimy fish bone at it. "Go away, bot. I don't need help."

The tutorial bot twirled and emitted a glow from its golden lines, continuing as if I hadn't said anything at all. "Selam, friend! You've indicated interest in joining the Hunt for Kaleb's Obelisk. Would you like to learn how to play?"

I groaned. I'd forgotten that level-one

participants *had* to run through a tutorial. Great. Besa sat on her haunches and cocked her head at the floating annoyance. I blew out a puff of frustration and tried to ignore it. Tutorial bots were only useful if you've never played the most popular game in the world since Solitaire 7.0. The floating pyramids could be found in-game to check your inventory, request assistance from a game admin, or even log a complaint against another player. But until the game started, they were long-winded nuisances, popping up where they weren't wanted and getting in the way.

"No," I said loudly. "I don't need to learn how to play. Go away. Please."

The bot twirled. "Excellent! You've selected 'Learn how to play'!"

"Teff of the saints! Go away!"

No such luck.

"King Kaleb," the bot began, "was a great king of Old Axum many centuries ago, but his grave was lost to history. It's said that whoever finds the obelisk that stands above it will be granted access to the treasures of Axum.

"The Hunt for Kaleb's Obelisk is the

world's greatest battle royale," the bot droned on. "Contestants must find the monument to the king while staying ahead of the Invasion, the ever-shrinking ring that reduces the competition area. You are allowed one approved in-game utility item. Two hundred and twenty-two players will compete to find golden talismans within each playing field before the time for the round runs out. No talisman, no entry to the next round. In the fifth and final round, the top two contestants will seek out one final golden talisman. Whoever holds the talisman when the timer runs out will be awarded top honors, including a prize of fifty thousand birr and the title of Addis Prime champion in the Hunt for Kaleb's Obelisk."

The bot paused, twirled, then asked cheerily, "Would you like to hear the tutorial again?"

I pinched the bridge of my nose, something I'd picked up from Uncle Moti when he was frustrated. "No. Please, no."

"Excellent! You've selected 'Hear the tutorial again'!"

"NO, YOU RUSTY PIECE OF

SCRAP! I DON'T WANT TO HEAR —"

"King Kaleb was a great king of Old . . ."

Ignoring the bot, I turned to Besa. "Forget it. Time to authenticate. Let's get this party started."

I rubbed my medallion for luck as Besa opened her mouth wide, wider than what might seem possible. From it emerged a projection that covered the opposite wall of the hovercan again. The HKO logo phased into view, a golden tower inside an ebony circle, before disappearing. My home away from home appeared on-screen, the place where everyone knew me and I wasn't constantly the new kid, reintroducing myself like a broken holo-vid. I had friends in the HKO. I was respected. Some days, that's all I had to look forward to.

"Authenticate," I said. I hesitated for a second, then sighed. "Yared Heywat."

The screen grew fuzzy. I held up both hands, not blinking. My fingerprints and eye pattern appeared in a laser grid, disintegrating into a string of characters too long to read. Then the whole screen into shapes that turned into letters. A title. One I'd seen a hundred times. No, a thousand. The title screen for my favorite game, the favorite of all of Addis Prime.

The Hunt for Kaleb's Obelisk.

I rubbed my hands as the authentication processed. The screen flashed red for a minute. My name appeared in bold. YARED HEYWAT, INACTIVE. ACCOUNT FLAGGED.

I pushed the button again, and the screen went green and the alert disappeared.

YARED HEYWAT, ACTIVE.

The HKO logo returned. "Welcome," said the cheery voice from Besa's speaker. "Prepare to join the Hunt!"

I grinned. It was time to play.

"What do you mean I have to wait to play?" I shouted.

I was standing in the alleys directly below the Gebeya, having abandoned the hovercan to continue on its way. And not a moment too soon. I was starting to smell like a two-day-old pot of fish.

Champions aren't supposed to stink!

The Gebeya's thrusters glowed like suns beneath the giant shopping district, the huge engines keeping the massive shopping mall aloft. I desperately wanted to be up there getting ready to hunt for the talismans. It was like a nagging itch I had to scratch. It worried at me, and —

Oh no, wait, that was a fish bone. I pulled it out and tossed it aside.

Haji pushed up his glasses and shook his head at me. "That's not what I said."

"You might as well have!" I took a step forward, then paused. Two giant kids stood on either side of Haji, arms folded. A boy and a girl. They towered over me like I was a toddler. Twins from the look of it. I didn't know their names but decided to call them Toe One and Toe Two. Because, well, they looked like toes.

"Do we have a problem?" Toe One asked.

Do you have a problem? I wanted to spit back. But that could lead to an argument, and maybe more, and I was trying to avoid trouble, not start it.

Rise above it, that's what Uncle Moti

always said. Even though he used to be a soldier, he hardly ever talked about that time in his past. He always preferred avoiding confrontation rather than causing a ruckus. I remember one time we were waiting outside our old flat for a market drone to deliver a new jar of mitmita. Uncle Moti refused to cook without it. Dinnertime wasn't complete without his red-stained fingerprints all over the tiny kitchenette, so he was pretty excited to get a new batch. But two coffee merchants got into a fight when their robotic bunamechs collided, and everyone was gathering around to watch. Uncle Moti got so flustered, he shouted that he would pay for both the coffee-ceremony bots to get repaired if they'd stop fighting.

Uncle Moti. Spending money just so someone *else* wouldn't fight. And he never got the mitmita he ordered. Talk about a sacrifice. If he could part with birr we didn't have to avoid conflict, I could bite my tongue and play nice. For now. I ignored the Toes and stared at Haji plaintively.

Haji sighed. "I said you couldn't enter

HKO alone. It's another one of the new rules this round. Look, Yared, I just found out about it, too. You have to partner up. The new sponsors are being real sticklers this time, I guess."

I stared at him in disbelief and groaned. It took a lot of server bandwidth to put on HKO, and servers meant money. A few companies recognized the revenue potential of a couple hundred kids competing in a virtual game, their exploits streamed to millions. Enter the sponsors, corporate partners that funneled money under the Authority's noses in exchange for strategic advertising in HKO.

NEWEST MODEL OF THE SKYLINE DRONE, SMALLER AND SLEEKER THAN EVER. DOWNLOAD COUPON.

LIMITED-EDITION SKYSAIL FOR HKO PLAYERS.

SHIELDS MADE FROM MENELIK DRIVES. LOOK LIKE AN ANCIENT WARRIOR.

Always something for sale.

But of course, that meant the sponsors thought they could mess with the rules, especially last minute.

"Partner?" I complained. "I don't have a partner. It's Yared the Great, not Yared the Great Plus One. C'mon, Haji, you know I fly solo. You can't do this to me. I'm —"

"If you're done complaining . . ." Haji blinked at me over the rim of his glasses, which kept sliding down his skinny nose. "Those are the rules. Besides, there are way too many new entrants from the server reset for solo play. So you have to team up or bow out. Now, I have somebody else who, like you, didn't know about the new rule and is late to the game. You two can pair up. Or you can always sit this one out and wait for the next game. Your choice."

"Your choice," Toe One repeated with a grunt.

"Yeah," said Toe Two.

I glared at them. Toes should be seen and not heard. But I couldn't worry about them. I had to make a choice. To be honest, I should've gone home. I should've turned around and walked back to Uncle Moti's place and put the whole thing behind me. That would've been the smart and safe thing to do. But

56

home . . . who knew how long we could afford even our small, cramped apartment? And if Uncle Moti had to shell out more money to keep me enrolled in that greedy, shady school . . .

My fingers balled into a fist. "Fine. Sign me up."

I mean, when have I ever done the smart and safe thing?

"Excellent," said Haji. But he looked nervous, like he didn't want to tell me something but he had to. He kept looking around, itchy, like he was expecting someone. "All right, while we wait for her to arrive —"

Her?

"— the scramble phrase is *Code White.* You hear that, you get out of there, got it?"

"Got it. Code White," I said, nodding impatiently. There was always a scramble phrase in place for HKO. It changed each game, and only the game admins could give it to you. Basically, if anything went wrong — Authority crackdown, server failure, or any number of things — the admins would flash the phrase in-game so only the players could see it. After that, it was everyone for themselves. Get out of there, find a place to lie low, and wait until the coast was clear. Standard stuff really.

Haji must've found what he was searching for, because he let out a giant, resigned sigh and adjusted his glasses. "Yared, here's the thing. Your partner —"

Uh-oh.

A whining sound cut through the air above us. I looked up in time to see the sleekest skysail shoot by, a figure leaping off the silver teardrop-shaped ship as it was still in motion. She flipped twice in the air, then landed on her hands and knees, like an action star from one of Uncle Moti's holopics I wasn't supposed to watch but totally did. (And if you snitch on me, I will stuff used exo grease down your shirt.)

She wore a tight-fitting hooded sweatshirt with a picture of a bird's wings on the back, and a cap with an emblem from the Awasa football team on the front. She stood and turned around slowly, all drama.

It was a girl about my age, with brown

skin and hair neatly coiled into curls on the top of her head. Amber eyes stared at me suspiciously from behind a strange bird-shaped mask that covered the bottom half of her face. She turned to Haji.

"Let's get this over with," she said in a low voice. Haji cleared his throat and motioned to me nervously.

"Perfect timing. Yared, meet your partner. The Ibis."

"No," I said.

This wasn't happening. This couldn't be happening. How was I supposed to write my name in the sky for all to see with the Ibis hanging around to steal my spotlight every chance she got?

It was impossible. Never going to happen. Not in a million years.

"No," I said again.

The Ibis turned in her seat next to me and frowned. "Would you stop saying that?"

"No."

"That's the only thing you've said since we left." She snorted, and the bird mask moved gently left to right as she shook her head in mock disbelief. "I already knew you were overrated. Didn't realize it was this bad. Just make sure you keep out of my way. I didn't come all this way just to lose because your feelings are hurt. And tell your aluminum cat to watch her tail. If that thing flicks me in the forehead one more time . . ."

We sat in the Ibis's skysail, flying a short distance away from where the Gebeya floated. The powered two-seater glider swayed in the air as Besa awkwardly shifted her weight back and forth. Ever the scaredy-cat.

Yes, we were high above Addis Prime, hundreds of meters away from the safety of the ground.

Yes, the squat apartments and winding streets lay far beneath us, squares of gray metal and dull green and drab brown stretching from one edge of the horizon to the other, like a blanket patched one too many times. Autos and kebele buses and hovercans and personal exos marched along like ants on thin gray lines that were the narrow roads.

Yes, we were very high.

I loved it. Another reason the Gebeya was so great — the no-fly restriction was lifted in its vicinity. What were you going to do, arrest the whole market? Everything about the place was fantastic. Except for Besa's cool claws digging into my neck as she tried to climb my head.

The air was thick and dusty. I pulled up my HKO glasses to rub at my eyes. Luckily, the Ibis and I both wore breathing masks. It was clearer a few meters down, but up here the dust and clouds kept us hidden from Authority patrols floating around the Gebeya, and out of the watching eyes of the Net.

Other HKO participants were doing the same. Every kid who could wriggle out of school, either by faking sick or taking a long lunch, was here. Even a few older teens had left secondary schools or their jobs to join in the competition. Every so often, a swirl of dust would dissipate to reveal the hull of another skysail, or moonsail, or even an old blocky tram. The free-floating elevators were testy things, but if you got one working, it could take an absolute pounding that you'd barely feel from inside.

I scowled at my new partner. Couldn't even control my face to keep from doing it. You've got to understand — the Ibis and I have a history. I first ran into her during a PvP free-for-all a couple years ago. This was before HKO really took off. Back then, battle royales were little more than augmented reality mosh pits. In those days, before the tournament transitioned to treasure hunts on foot, you dropped in, piloted digital exos around a crowded valley, and tried to disable as many other exos as you could before someone got yours.

It was chaos.

It was destruction.

I loved it.

Piloting the exos was such a rush. Massive three-meter-tall armored suits packed with antigrav thrusters, they streaked through the air as you raced to the valley floor. Sitting inside one, even if it was only a digital version, was unlike anything you'd ever seen. Holographic overlays showed the outside world in incredible detail, and with the flip of a switch, I could leap thirty meters into the air before you could blink. They were incredible.

I'd perfected the technique of taking out enemy exos before we'd even landed, and the confusion below separated the champs from the chumps. Before you knew it, I'd wrecked your existence and kicked you out of the game. Easy.

That is, until the Ibis came along and knocked me off my block. For the first time in a long time, someone called me out and backed it up. But don't tell anyone. I don't like to admit it.

Now I looked at her again and shook my head. I tried to think of something mean to say, but she'd slipped on a pair of earphones and was nodding her head to a beat only she could hear. I settled for a glare. *As soon as I catch the first talisman, I'll set off on my own,* I thought.

Drones buzzed around the outside of the Gebeya like flies near rotten meat. Two-rotors, quad-rotors — I even spotted an octo-rotor that was larger than a bus. Its eight rotor blades spun in a blur above it as it carried crates larger than me to the very top of the marketplace.

I licked my lips. The signal would come soon. I was seconds away from launching my legend. The moment I dreamed of. Fame. Glory. My name written in the sky for the world to see. All of it would be mine.

All I had to do was find the talismans.

Okay, it was a bit more difficult than that. But simple plan, simple reward, as Uncle Moti always said. I went over the steps to my eventual success to get my mind off the lecture and punishment I'd get if he found out I was here. When I won, I'd have plenty of birr, and that would at least keep some of his griping to a minimum.

I mapped out the market in my head, guessing at where the talismans might be. In the beginning, there would be plenty of them to go around; you just had to search the playing area. They'd be hidden in pipes or on top of merchant stalls, that sort of thing.

Near the end, as the competition whittled down and more and more kids got knocked out, only a few paltry talismans would be generated, the numbers dwindling each round.

And for the last stage — it was time to battle for the last talisman. Two players would make it in, but only one champion would be crowned.

Fight!

"Are you and the glitter kitty ready?" The Ibis didn't turn around when she spoke, and for a second, I didn't realize she was talking to me. But then again, we were floating in a tiny hovering vehicle, packed so tight that I felt like I could practically hear her thoughts. Who else was she going to talk to?

"Besa and I were born ready," I shot back. "Well, *I* was. She was created ready. Built ready? I think —"

"Okay, okay. I'm sorry I asked." She pointed to a spot just in front of the center of the Gebeya.

I didn't see anything. The Ibis shook her head in annoyance and tapped her HKO glasses. I flushed, pulling mine down over my eyes. A thrill of excitement raced along my skin.

A flowing script materialized, as if a giant unseen hand had traced calligraphy in the sky. Golden letters swept across my vision before transforming into a dazzling orange-red color, as if the words were written in the sunset.

My fingers clenched. I leaned forward in excitement as the message was broadcast through Besa's speaker.

"Welcome, travelers . . .

Who will be the first to reach their goal?

Can you stay ahead of the Invasion?

The Hunt for Kaleb's Obelisk begins . . .

NOW!"

We zoomed around the Gebeya, slicing through the clouds.

"Beetles on the left!" I shouted.

"I see them," she said.

Rumor had it the beetle drones got their nickname because the older Authority Net drone models weren't able to fly if they flipped upside down. If you managed to knock one topsy-turvy with a large stick or a well-aimed rock, the drone would crash to the ground and wriggle on its back like a beetle. The name stuck. Of course, newer models corrected the issue, but sometimes a good nickname can't be undone.

Sort of like Yared TheGr8, right?

. . .

Right?

Anyway.

Shoppers and merchants alike glared at us, but they didn't see what we saw. Winged guardians with slashing tails and vicious scepters tried to squash us. Doors of neon light tried to lead us into walls, while meteors rained down and burst like sparklers in front of our faces. All the while, other players tried to find a way to the next round just like we did.

"Try beneath it!" I yelled.

"No. They wouldn't put them near the thrusters. At least not yet."

"How do you know —"

But she'd already whipped the skysail left, cutting off ten other players in one swoop, and made a nosedive for a nearby corridor. "Bet they're in the stalls." She parked her skysail. It was nice, but it wasn't my nefasi. She swept her fingers in a complicated pattern on the glider's hull and . . .

"Where did it go?" I asked. The skysail had faded from view. Sort of. I could still kind of see it if I relaxed my eyes and didn't try to focus. A hazy outline appeared, like a bubble shaped like a ship.

"Keep your voice down," she whispered. "Camouflage. Just in case *someone* gets any ideas."

She didn't look at me when she said that, but I knew she was talking about me. But while I was trying to come up with a retort, she hissed a warning and pulled me down into a crouch behind a metal recycler.

We crouched in a narrow alcove.

"What's your real name?" I asked. "I'm not going to go on calling you the Ibis. Like, that's not a name."

"I don't know you," she replied.

"Hi, Yared the Great, future winner. Now you're supposed to return the favor."

"Am I? You could be lying."

She ducked, and I mimicked her as other game players raced through the area, quickly moving on. "Get behind me so people can't see you."

I rolled my eyes. "You're the one in the bird mask," I said under my breath. Besa and I tucked ourselves between a woman selling colorful candies and a baker's counter piled high with crispy seasoned puffs. The HKO filter turned them into a duo of angry, sword-wielding guards, with flames for eyes and a mountain of magical missiles between them.

I loved this game.

"The coast is clear." The Ibis's whisper floated back to me in my hiding spot.

I tapped Besa's side, and we crept out.

This area of the Gebeya spilled over with food vendors. The aromas were incredible. Wat, shiro, sambusas — my growling stomach nearly gave us away on three occasions. As it was about lunchtime, the other shopkeepers made their way to the wide array of food and drink stalls to unwind, and conversations and laughter filled the air.

It was busy.

Maybe too busy.

Drones buzzed over our heads, and assistants carried requests and deliveries everywhere. I'd intended to split off from the Ibis and slip away. But before I could: "Hey —" she called out, grabbing the back of my shirt. "Look."

There, at the end of the passageway, past a woman selling ground peppers, was a talisman, floating unnoticed. It spun gently above a partially collapsed skysail shop that had definitely seen better days. The talisman was stunning, a carving made of wood black as night and inlaid with silver.

Yes, the Ibis had spotted it first. But I probably would've seen it, too, if she hadn't insisted on being in the front. We had to get it. It was calling our — I mean my — name.

But surrounding it? Five heavily armored Authority troopers. Addis Prime's security forces normally hunted down criminals. Thieves, swindlers, that sort of thing. But recently they'd been combing the streets and interrogating citizens, even innocent market pedestrians and merchants. These five were on high alert, shock-batons out as they watched and waited . . . for something.

Was the game going to be shut down before it even started? I pounded a fist softly into my hand. Did they know about it?

It wasn't fair!

Merchants and vendors gave the Authority a wide berth, keeping their heads down and hurrying on their way. More than a few stopped short when they saw the troopers and walked in the opposite direction. I didn't blame them. The Authority had the unique talent of "finding" something wrong even if all your papers were in order and you'd been on your best behavior. They made it their business to dole out fines, and occasionally threats of far worse. If you were a group of kids playing an illegal virtual game in a space reserved for permit-holding adults . . . well, it wouldn't be pretty.

Still . . . something seemed off.

"Why aren't they patrolling?" I whispered. "It's like they're waiting for something in particular."

The Ibis turned to me. "What? Of course they aren't —"

Before she could finish, one of the

troopers stiffened and dropped to a crouch. She grunted — a large container was bolted to her back, and it opened slowly. I couldn't see what was inside, but whatever it was, the troopers seemed enraptured by it.

All of a sudden, they turned as one — looking straight at our hiding place. "The Bulgu is here," one called, and instantly the other four stood. The trooper with the semi-opened container growled something beneath her breath and then slowly stood, the container closing. "Secure the exits."

The Bulgu? Like the monster from Uncle Moti's stories? But I didn't have time to think about it any longer as the troopers were marching straight toward us. I held my breath. The Ibis tensed. One of the troopers stopped right next to us. A gloved hand reached down, inches away from where Besa's tail tried to curl up and shrink. If the trooper just glanced to the right, we were history.

But instead, he grabbed a still-steaming doughnut off the floor, grunted, and tucked it away.

Was he really going to eat that later?

That was just nasty. But to my relief, he and the other troopers kept on walking.

I exhaled softly — then froze.

The HKO talisman still floated there invitingly. Before I could talk myself out of what I was pretty sure was the worst idea ever, I crept forward on my hands and knees, right out of our hiding place.

Bad idea, bad idea, bad idea.

A sharp intake of breath came from behind me, followed by a low yowl of frustration. Great. My two teammates were bonding over their shared disapproval of my bold move.

I inched my way along. The overhang of a few of the stalls offered some cover, but there was a clear space about three paces wide separating me from the talisman . . . and the backs of the tyrant troopers. I took a deep breath and slipped out into the open.

One step at a time.

Tiptoe.

Don't breathe. Don't look. Don't even think about them.

Just a few . . . more . . . inches . . .

Through the HKO glasses, my hands gripped the talisman. I let out a silent sigh of relief. But as I turned around, the key to the next stage began to twist, gold and silver light erupting out of it, filling the area with digital brilliance.

I froze.

The talisman glitched once, then twice, before morphing into the shape of a lion.

That was strange. It almost looked like . . .

I pulled my medallion from beneath my shirt and stared at it. It *was* the same. Down to the same gold outline, the same frozen expression as if it had been caught midroar. They were even the same size. I held them closer together, just to compare . . .

The talisman glitched, then disappeared into my medallion. Seconds later, a voice boomed out of Besa's speaker.

"MENELIK DRIVES ONLINE."

I froze for an instant, then started to back up. Oh no. I needed to get to the hiding place before —

I bumped into something solid. I

reached back and felt behind me. Boots. Armor. Uh-oh. I turned around slowly. An Authority trooper stood over me. He lifted his visor. Bright golden eyes peered out at me, cold and calculating. We stared at each other for several tense and breathless seconds.

"Um . . . hi," I said. "Fine day, isn't it?"

He didn't answer. Instead, he lifted his hand. A virtual screen appeared above it, where a face stared out, wide-eyed with a snaggle-toothed grin. I heard a whining hiss, then realized all the breath had rushed out of my lungs.

It was my class picture from several years back.

They were looking for me!

The trooper reached down to grab me —

— only to fall away when an enormous boom rocked the Gebeya.

Everyone in the market crashed to the ground as the wall behind the exos exploded. The entire surface peeled outward, like the skin of a melon.

A massive roar shook the space, toppling stalls, sending platters of spices spilling everywhere and bowls of steaming wat and injera splattering across the floor. I rolled over as drones smashed into the ground and into each other. The air filled with screams and shrieks. The very core of the floating district seemed to wobble, and I tumbled head over heels toward the opening in the wall.

Empty air stretched before me. Endless, floating, flying.

"Oomph!"

I slammed into the corner pole of a stall and just managed to grab on. Still, the air was punched out of my lungs. The walls of a fruit stand crumpled around me, so that it looked like I was dangling over a large bowl. Beneath it, an opening about the size of a hovercan waited to suck me down into the vast emptiness beneath the Gebeya as soon as I let go. Debris and rubble fell out, along with fluttering reams of cloth and shiny exo parts.

"Yared!" the Ibis screamed.

Above me, she and Besa stood atop a now-sideways stall and stared down in horror.

"I'm fine!" I shouted. "Just . . . hang-ing in there."

"No, watch out for —"

Another roar shook the Gebeya. I peeked down and nearly let go from fear.

A massive metal eye peered at me through the hole in the wall.

Audio Transcript File No. 2132.055

Location: [UNDISCLOSED DETENTION FACILITY]

Time: 02:00

Subject: Yared [LAST NAME REDACTED FOR SECURITY]

Auditor: So . . .

Me: Hey, can I have a cup of tea?

Auditor: Sit down and be quiet. Let's talk about your infiltration team.

Me: My what now?

Auditor: [RUSTLING PAPERS] That partner of yours will crack soon, and the bionic . . . creature . . . you brought with you.

Me: I don't know what you're talking about.

Auditor: It seems repeated EMP blasts will gradually wear down the cat's diranium shielding, but —

Me: IF YOU'VE HARMED ONE METALLIC HAIR ON BESA'S HEAD, I WILL USE YOUR SKULL TO GRIND MY COFFEE!

Auditor: . . .

Me: . . .

Me: I'm sorry, that was rude. No need for the restraints. I'll behave now.

Auditor: I'm starting to get the impression you think this is a game.

Me: And I'm starting to think I'm not getting any tea.

Auditor: Did they teach you to evade questioning? Who trained you?

Me: Who is this "they"?

Auditor: . . .

Auditor: I will get answers out of you one way or the other.

Me: But will I get any tea?

CHAPTER THREE

If time flies when you're having fun, it slows to a crawl when you stare death in the eye.

Its giant, unblinking . . . robotic eye? Sounds about right.

Screams still echoed throughout the Gebeya as fruits and vegetables and clouds of spices fell all around us. The market stalls were twisted and bent, and someone groaned in pain nearby. The Authority troopers from earlier were nowhere to be found. My HKO glasses somehow remained perched on my face, and the game's servers registered nearly a third of the competitors as disconnected. Everything was in shambles. I heard ringing in my left ear. Time was inching forward.

And through it all, that giant, blistering-red eye watched my hiding place. My arms were starting to tremble as I tried not to bump the sides of the empty produce canister I dangled inside. It smelled like citrus. Oranges, maybe? Lovely. At least the monster wouldn't get scurvy as it ate me alive.

My fingers gripped the lip of the container, its sharp edge biting into my flesh. Something rumbled below, and I held my breath. Through a peek hole I saw the giant eye narrow. Something rumbled again, a growl that shook the entire Gebeya. Then the creature disappeared from view.

I let out a sigh of relief.

"Yared?"

The whisper came from above me. Who — Oh right. The Ibis. She crouched on top of a damaged clothing stall. Besa shifted in frustration next to her. My lioness yowled softly as she saw me inside the canister. I flashed a shaky grin as I tried to maintain my grip on the canister, then slowly pulled myself out.

"I'm fine," I said, wincing as I shook my fingers. Everything ached. I felt like something had chewed me up and spit me out. Actually, if we didn't find an exit fast, that was still a possibility.

The Ibis must have been thinking the same thing as she looked around. "We have to leave, now."

"Agreed. It'd be nice to reach solid ground."

"Without getting caught."

"That, too." I looked around. "Where's your invisible skysail? It'd sure come in handy."

The Ibis surveyed the crumpled hallways, wrinkling her nose at the smelly exhaust coming from between cracks in the floor. (Or were they the walls now?) A Menelik drive must have been damaged. Hopefully only one. If two got damaged, the Gebeya might start to drop out of the sky. Ever see a ship crash to the ground? Multiply it by a hundred. Yeah. No one wanted to see that.

"I think . . ." the Ibis started to say, then pursed her lips. "I think it's up there." She pointed high above the dozens of stalls now stacked precariously on top of one another, to where a couple had smashed together. A fish stall and another selling berbere spice. Rivulets of stinky fish water swirled with the bright red piles to form a pungent paste that looked like it could stain air. It dripped down and covered everything, but it also conveniently formed a trail to guide us out. At the top of the stream, a cramped tunnel led up and out of view.

Now it was my turn to wrinkle my nose. I clambered to join her and Besa on top of the stall. "There is no way I'm squeezing through that mess. I'd rather d—"

A metallic hiss, something I'd never heard before, came out of Besa's speakers. She was crouched down, belly flat to the stall's surface. Her tail twitched in agitation, and her claws were fully extended.

But what surprised me even more were the two ridges of spikes that now emerged from her back, bristling like spears as she stared behind me. My jaw dropped. Since when did Besa have spikes?

"Besa, what's —"

SMASH.

The section of the Gebeya where I'd

just been hiding disappeared in a cloud of metal shards and noxious smoke. The impact sent us tumbling, while the billowing fumes stung my eyes. I rubbed at them furiously as Besa continued to hiss. When I could finally see, tears streaming down my face, I wished I'd never opened my eyes.

A massive, corroded metal hand, the claws fused together and flared out like an ax head, reached up through a gaping hole.

Stinky fish paste it was.

"Go!" I shouted, leaping up and catching the edge of the next sideways stall, pulling myself up and scrambling onto a stack of melons to reach a ledge. "Climb!"

Another huge roar shook the Gebeya. Someone screamed as the Ibis, Besa, and I scrabbled along overturned market stalls, sometimes leaping from one to another across a dizzying drop when our path upward was blocked. Below, the monstrous eye glared at us through the ever-widening hole as the ax-hand ripped the corridor to metal shreds.

"Go, go, go!" The Ibis extended a hand

and I grabbed it, and we helped each other reach the twisted tunnel of metal. Besa clawed her way in first, gouging the surface as she struggled to find footing. I looked down, then immediately regretted it. The ax was getting closer. This monster — whatever it was — was destroying everything in its path as it homed in on our position.

"I think your cat is stuck!" the Ibis shouted.

I whipped around, then groaned. Besa was wedged into the tunnel, blocking our only escape. Her strange new spikes had gotten lodged in the tunnel of debris, and her rear paws kicked fishy paste back at us. But that was the least of our worries. The Gebeya was shuddering every few seconds, and my stomach lurched each time it did. If the giant clawed monster didn't crush us, the market hurtling to the ground certainly would.

Besa yowled.

"I don't know, shimmy or something," I said. A glob of paste zipped past me. "Watch it! You're getting it . . ." I paused, then grimaced as the answer to our problems splattered onto my clothes.

"Everywhere. We need to get it every-where. We'll squeeze through easier . . . I hope." I scooped up the slimy red paste and smeared it onto Besa's exposed sides.

"Hurry up," the Ibis warned. Fear colored her voice. I could hear the monster getting closer. The stall we stood on shuddered as one of the claws punctured it. The metal squealed, and I gulped.

"There," I said, slapping on one more coat. "Try it now!"

Besa hissed, wiggled, then popped through. I let out a crow of triumph.

"Yes! Yared the Great is *still* great."

"*And* still stinky," the Ibis corrected, before moving past me and climbing up into the tunnel.

I started to snap off a witty reply (trust me, it was going to be epic), but the monster roared below me. I peered over the edge. The bottom of this section of the Gebeya was gone. Disappeared. There was a hole the size of a hovercan that led to open air, and beneath it sat the ugliest, meanest, scariest-looking robotic creature I'd ever seen.

The head of a snapping turtle.

Multiple rows of jagged shark teeth.

Four legs.

Ax heads at the end of each foot.

And two glowing red eyes.

The Bulgu. It couldn't be. The monster from Uncle Moti's stories . . . it was real?

It saw me. One of its eyes narrowed until it looked like a pinprick. Then the beast threw back its head and let out a roar that nearly deafened me. The walls shook and my teeth rattled. The Bulgu raised itself on its hind legs and extended its gleaming fused claw again.

That was my cue to leave.

I leapt for the opening just as the claw swiped at the stall I'd been standing on, obliterating it in a shower of sparks and metal. I clambered up into the tunnel, sliding through oozing fish spice paste. After what seemed like forever, I slid out the other side. The Ibis, sitting on her skysail with Besa perched on the back, held out a hand. I grabbed it and hopped on board.

"Let's get out of here," she called back to me.

I nodded, but my attention was elsewhere. As we zoomed out of the Gebeya, I felt the Ibis inhale sharply and heard Besa whine. I felt the same way.

The giant floating market was wrecked. The bottom was completely gone. Groans of pain and cries for help fluttered through the destruction. So many injured. I couldn't see them. From here it sounded like the Gebeya itself was dying. The marvel of Addis Prime, battered and leaking debris. And for what?

As I stared at the three-story monster still rooting through the wreckage, a little voice inside me answered the question.

It's looking for you, Yared.

"What was that thing?"

The Ibis didn't look at me as she piloted the skysail around the outskirts of Addis Prime. In the distance, far to the northwest, old factories the size of small mountains lined up along the foothills of an actual mountain. The brooding, massive Ghebbi Fortress loomed at the top. Four giant peaks stabbed upward through the clouds and into the sky. Rumor had it that you could hike from the foothills, up through the mountains, and all the way to the stars if you were disciplined and knew the way. At least, that's what Uncle Moti always said.

Right now, I needed Uncle Moti to tell me what to do next.

We'd flown fast and low, out of range of the Authority drones in the sky, as far north as we could go before the mountain range cut us off. Then we circled east. Uncle Moti and I lived outside the city in the deserted factory district. I was hesitant at first to give the Ibis directions to my home, but there was no way I could make it there on foot. And after today's events, I just needed to get somewhere safe, fast. It was the only thing I could think of. Couldn't go back to the school after the destruction of the Gebeya. Everyone would be on high alert. No way I'd be able to sneak back in, nefasi or not. I just hoped Uncle Moti wouldn't yell at me.

The Ibis finally glanced back at me, one of her eyebrows raised. She wanted an answer.

I shook my head. "I don't know what it was."

"Well, what are we going to do now?"

"I don't know," I repeated. Besa shifted beside me, and the frown I wore deepened. The strange, twin spiky ridges running down either side of her back were still there. I touched one, then hissed in pain and shook my finger. Those things were sharp! I stared at them and sighed. After nearly getting caught by Authority guards and then running from an enormous monster tearing apart the Gebeya, Besa's dangerous new accessories should've sent me into a spiraling panic. Instead, I just felt . . . tired.

"What's wrong with her?"

I looked up to see the Ibis still staring back at us. "I don't know."

"Wow, do you know anything?" she asked, rolling her eyes. I glared at her, my hand on Besa's side, though I was careful to avoid the spikes. It brought to mind the comments the headmistress made earlier this morning, and a wave of fury swept through me.

"Actually, I do. I know how to load a self-replicating simulation into an Authority drone that will burn out its logic circuit board. I know Ms. Eden always leaves a plate of fresh sambusas outside her back window for kids who might be hungry but don't have money for meals. I know all the channels the Authority uses to coordinate their so-called random sweeps. And I know the best insults in seven different languages, like this one: You're a —"

Besa growled and shouldered me before settling down on her haunches.

"I wasn't really going to say it," I muttered. I looked at the Ibis. "The point *is* . . . I've seen a lot and done a lot, but I've never seen anything like what happened back there."

The Ibis shook her head. "Those things were looking for you! The Authority, that giant turtle-looking monster . . . all of them." The skysail banked sharply without warning as the Ibis veered behind a series of hills, keeping out of the open air. She brought us to a hover above a wild field of teff, the vibrations of the skysail bending the large reddish-brown stalks backward. Birds erupted out of hiding and took to the sky.

"Don't pretend like you didn't notice. One of the suits had a picture of you!

What did you get me into? Are you a criminal or something?"

"Of course not," I snapped.

"Well, what about your family — did they do anything? Are your parents crime bosses or something? Do you all steal hovercans together?"

"Now you're being ridiculous." I stared at Besa, but not really looking at her. Instead, all the instances where I had to pick up and move in the middle of the night replayed in my head. Could . . . ? No, I refused to entertain it. "Besides, it's just me and Uncle Moti."

"You all live all the way out here?"

I looked out the domed shield of the skysail. "Yeah."

"Where are your parents?"

I didn't answer. After a second, the Ibis looked away. "Sorry," she said.

The teff outside rippled in the skysail's exhaust, like purple waves crashing on an alien beach. But I couldn't focus on the beauty. Uncle Moti never really talked about my parents. The one time I asked he got really upset, only telling me that they fought a losing war. He kept a picture of them in a password-locked vid-screen he never let out of his sight.

Last year on his birthday, Uncle Moti invited a couple old friends over, and they sipped coffee and stayed up late into the night talking about times long past. When I woke up and came to get a drink of water, I discovered Uncle Moti was showing them the vidscreen. I briefly saw an elegant couple standing together, tall and proud, before Uncle Moti caught me looking.

That was the only time I ever saw my uncle cry.

Besa rumbled next to me, dragging me out of my memories. My uncle always had an explanation for everything, a solution for every problem, which usually came with some story about the good old days . . . I needed that right about now.

And a change of clothes. It was starting to smell like two-day-old garbage.

"Okay," I said. "Just drop me off there, at the last factory on the opposite side of the hills. I need to talk to my uncle. He should know what to do."

The Ibis looked at me skeptically, but

she pushed forward on the controls, sending the skysail rushing upward. I figured she was itching to get home, too. After everything that happened, we all needed something familiar. We skimmed above the tops of the teff and grass and colorful wildflowers dotting the hillsides, keeping low as we zipped around several abandoned factories. Finally, a lone building remained — three stories high, rusted brown and gray, the giant bay doors wide open.

"Gotta say, I love what you've done with the place." The Ibis squinted. "Suppose it could be worse. At least you don't have neighbors. Or siblings. My sisters are always waking up super early on the weekends, and I swear they hold dance parties with giraffes because —"

"Wait," I said.

"— they stomp around like they don't have any toes to tip around on! And don't get me started on —"

"Wait!"

"What?"

Besa yowled in distress as I lunged forward and yanked down on the flight controls. The skysail dropped like a stone, landing with a jarring thump just below the crest of a hill covered in bushes.

"Hey!" The Ibis shoved me away, glaring but holding off from leaping across the seats to attack, probably because Besa had inserted herself between the two of us. Though from the way the lioness was baring her teeth at *me,* she was none too happy about the sudden landing, either. "That's it! Get out. I'm done with you."

"Something's wrong," I said. My voice caught, and I think it was that more than anything that grabbed the Ibis's attention.

"What?"

"The doors. Uncle Moti never opens the bay doors. They're always getting stuck, and then undertaker birds get inside, Besa starts chasing them, and — well, we never open the bay doors. Something's wrong." I sat up slowly, and all three of us stared out the window at the shadowy interior of the old factory. Something winked inside, like light glinting off glass. A reflection?

The Ibis and I reached the same conclusion mere seconds apart. We glanced at each other, speaking in hushed tones at the same time.

"The Authority."

I started down the slope toward the factory, when the Ibis grabbed my arm.

"What are you doing?" she whispered.

Besa was slinking off through the grass as well, moving at an angle that kept the factory in sight while keeping low to the ground. I pointed after her. "My uncle is down there. If he's in trouble, I have to do something."

The Ibis stared at me as if I'd sprouted a tail. "Do what? Get arrested?"

"He's my *uncle.* The only person I have in this world. I can't just leave him there."

The Ibis shook her head. "And what would he say?"

I hesitated. She did have a point. I could hear Uncle Moti's raspy voice now as he folded his arms over the greasy jumpsuit he always wore and stared down at me over his glasses. *Foolish boy.*

What could I do? I watched as Besa's tail — the only part of her I could see as she moved stealthily through the tall grass — flicked in the air. An idea popped into my head.

I pulled out the HKO glasses and pried off the tiny panel on the corner of the frame, right below the black-and-gold letters. A small circuit board rested there, with tiny wires leading to the lenses. I grinned and pulled out my toolkit. This was a challenge I could handle.

"What are you doing?" The Ibis leaned over my shoulder.

I paused. She *was* my main competitor in the HKO after all. Did I really want her knowing every one of my tricks? My advantages? I squinted at her with suspicion, and she blinked at me innocently. Then a crash sounded from inside the warehouse, and we both jumped. My heart started pounding. I sighed. What was an advantage in a game if I lost someone I cared about in real life?

"I . . ." Wow, this was hard to explain. "I'm reprogramming the HKO glasses. Going to bypass the locks for the virtual inputs and reroute them to the ocular transmitter I built for Besa. Then I'll engage the subvocal comms unit."

The Ibis nodded. "So you can see what she sees, and she can hear your instructions."

I stared at her. "Right."

"What? You think I wouldn't understand? Because I'm a girl?"

"What? No, of course not, I just . . ."

"Save it. In fact, splice that wire right there and clip it to the partner link relay in the upper corner. That way *I* can see, too. Partner." The Ibis folded her arms as I gawked at her. After a few seconds, she stuck out her tongue. It was a move so childish I snorted, and a small grin crept across her face.

Say what you want, everybody needs a good rival.

I finished the alterations, and we each slipped on our glasses. "Here goes nothing," I muttered.

The view from the crest of the hill disappeared, replaced by a black-and-white image of tall stalks of grass. The front corner of the warehouse was just visible above them. As we watched, Besa crept forward, constantly scanning the area for trouble. She eased up to the warehouse, then leapt into the air, clinging to the wall. Silently, she began to climb.

"Where is she going?" the Ibis asked.

"I never use the doors," I whispered back. "There's a window on the second floor that Besa normally drops a ladder from. Or there's an old conveyor belt system that we'll ride up. Oh, and there's a garbage chute that Uncle Moti and I converted into an elevator. I call it the stealthy-vator, but it hasn't caught on with Uncle Moti yet. Not sure why."

The Ibis didn't say anything for a while. Then: "Why all the secrecy?"

"Well —" I paused, then thought about it. "I . . . don't know, actually. That's just how it's always been."

"You know that's not normal, right? Having secret entrances? It's like you have something to hide. Like . . . that's pretty weird."

"No it isn't. You don't know what you're talking about."

The Ibis sighed. "I'm not the one whose home is being raided."

I didn't have a response to that. Luckily, Besa had reached the window and slipped inside, so I could turn my attention to finding my uncle. A balcony ran around the inside of the warehouse, with a set of stairs that climbed up to the third floor. That was where I stashed all my stuff I didn't want Uncle Moti looking at. I made a note to check that nothing was taken later, but right now I only had eyes for the chaos unfolding on the main floor below.

When we first moved into the warehouse, Uncle Moti and I had spent weeks outfitting the place to suit our needs. I chased out small animals and swept while Uncle Moti hooked the place up with power and purchased second-hand furniture. We turned the first floor into the coolest studio apartment ever. At the time it had seemed like a fun game. Installing five sets of ultra-secure locks on the doors. Putting an alarm system in my bedroom. Building a trapdoor beneath a very specific couch cushion. Security bots that looked like rats. Fun! Now, as I stared at the dozens of guards swarming around the first floor, overturning furniture and dumping the contents of Uncle Moti's workbench, I began to get a nervous feeling in the pit of my stomach. And that feeling intensified when I saw the two troopers wearing power armor, their thrusters idling in the middle of the room. Exos.

"Besa," I whispered, "maybe you should —"

Just then, one of the guards turned and looked up, scanning the room. A finger touched the side of his white helmet, like someone was telling him where to look. The visor on the helmet raised, and a pair of narrowed eyes looked around. Besa zoomed in without me needing to ask, and the Ibis gasped beside me.

The golden-eyed man from the Gebeya.

The man held up a gloved hand, and all the activity in the room stopped. Slowly, his fingers curled into a fist. "We have an intruder." He spoke in a smooth voice that rooted me in place.

As one, every soldier pulled out a wicked-looking curved sword. As we watched, the blades seemed to ripple in the air. No Authority trooper carried weapons like that — where were the stun sticks? And the Authority rode around in little hovering tuk-tuks. Not exo mechs. These weren't real troopers . . . they were impostors.

"Yared," the Ibis whispered.

"I saw," I said, my mind racing.

"What are they doing? The Authority aren't supposed to bring weapons to security checks."

I swallowed. "Those aren't Authority guards. They're the same people from the Gebeya, and those aren't just weapons. They're shotels. How they got them is a whole different question. Uncle Moti told me about them." I racked my brain, trying to remember what he'd said. "He told me a story about a war, where the weapons of the Axum were stolen and turned against them. *The Black Fire* he called them. Those blades will slice through me, you, and even a two-ton exo with ease. They burn through circuits like dry grass."

"Wait, your uncle knew about these . . . these swords?"

I shook my head. "They were just stories. The shotels. The creature back at the Gebeya. He would tell me bedtime stories about them, and the kingdom in the sky, Axum. Just . . . fables."

Except they weren't. Everything I thought I knew was unraveling before my eyes. It was hard to understand, but living it out in real time was rapidly making me a believer.

Suddenly, the golden-eyed trooper, who I was starting to suspect was the leader, spun around and glared up in the air . . . *right where Besa was crouching!*

"There." He pointed. Without question, the two soldiers in exos took off, their exhaust sending papers rustling everywhere. They zoomed through the air, heading for Besa's hiding spot on the balcony. They cocked their shotel swords back, ready to slice my lioness in half.

"BESA, GET OUT OF THERE!" I screamed.

Golden Eyes smiled, a cruel twist in his lips. He turned and strode out the warehouse doors. The rest of the troops followed.

"Oh no," the Ibis whispered.

I yanked off my glasses to find she had done the same. We peeked over the hill.

Twisting, slithering tendrils of cold fear spread throughout my body as I realized my mistake. The impostor soldiers exited the warehouse at a run, and they were headed straight for us.

"We need to leave — now," I said. The Ibis didn't answer. I saw a cat-shaped shadow leap out of the warehouse window and streak through the grass, and I let out a shaky breath —

— only to inhale sharply when the side of the warehouse exploded outward as the shotel-wielding exos cut through the walls.

"Yeah, we need to go!"

Again, no answer from the Ibis.

I turned around and froze.

A battered old exo loomed before me, its tinted helmet hiding the pilot inside. It stood on rusted legs, and the upper frame bulged outward, like it had a refrigerator bolted to its chest plate. Smoke wisped out from its joints. At some point, it had been painted every color under the sun — yellow, sky blue, even violet! It was the ugliest exoskeleton I'd ever seen in my life.

But — and this was probably more important than how it looked — it held one hand over the Ibis's mouth. The other held a massive recurved warbow, and the terribly sharp cone-shaped arrows with blinking laser sights on them looked to be in perfect condition.

That was aimed straight at me.

The exo leaned forward. "Get up. Now."

CHAPTER FOUR

Shouts echoed behind me. The battered exo turned its helmet to look, then returned its gaze to me. Then, to my complete surprise, the hand holding the Ibis released her, gently pushing her toward me. It spoke again.

"I said, get up. Get in your vessel and follow me. Do exactly as I do, and do not stop for anything. Understand?"

The warbow jerked to the skysail. The Ibis looked left and right, ready to flee in any other direction. "Yared, what are they saying?"

I stared at her, confused, then quickly looked back at the exo. The pilot hadn't been speaking Amharic! What dialect was that . . . ? Neo-Somalian. No. Wait, it couldn't be . . . ?

"They . . . want us to get in the skysail.

I think. My Afar — yes, that *was* Afar — it's a bit rusty, but I'm pretty sure they want us to follow."

"You understood that?"

I nodded shakily. Before I could explain about Uncle Moti's lessons, more shouts came from the other side of the hill. The stand of high teff behind us rattled, and I tensed. Then Besa slid out, claws digging furrows into the hill. She came to a stop beside me, collapsing at my feet. A huge, gaping slash ran across her flank. Oil and hydraulic gel gushed out every time she limped forward on her paws.

"Besa!" I dropped to my knees. There was another scratch running across her jaw, and more than a few dents covered her back. Some of the spines had fallen out or gotten bent. She was injured. My hands trembled as I struggled with what to do next. Finally, I just hugged her, spikes or not.

"Time is running out, little warriors." The exo's thrusters engaged, sending puffs of black smoke everywhere. Besa cocked her head in my arms, and then — shocking me even further — she struggled to her feet and stumbled up to the exo. She nuzzled it and then looked back at me, as if to say, *What are you waiting for?*

"Fine," I said, wiping my tears. The Ibis and I somehow managed to lift the heavy lioness into the skysail. The mysterious exo pilot followed, and once we'd hopped inside, the Ibis engaged thrusters and took off. Seconds later we were airborne. The exo shot straight upward, and we trailed behind it. We rose higher and higher, and none too soon. The impostor soldiers swarmed over the hill, then stopped as they saw us soaring into the sky. Through the window, I saw Golden Eyes point and two exo-wearing soldiers leapt into the air, their shotels aimed toward us.

"Remember!" The Ibis and I jumped as the word boomed inside the skysail. It was the stranger we were following. But how . . . ?

"Stay close! Don't fall behind." And with that, the battered exo lifted the warbow and fired.

A silver bolt streaked across the sky. Just as the arrow reached the two enemy pursuers, it exploded in what looked like a glittering cloud of dust and confetti.

"Really?" I muttered. "Are we escaping or trying to start a party?"

The sound of a snort echoed through the skysail. The Ibis and I exchanged glances. The exo pilot could hear us!

"No," the stranger said. "It's a chaff arrow. Confuses their targeting systems."

"Look!" the Ibis shouted, pointing below us. The impostor Authority exos were going haywire — jerking left, plummeting a couple of meters, then twirling and heading full speed in the opposite direction.

"Now," the voice said, "follow me, quickly." The stranger took off. The Ibis hesitated, then engaged the controls and sent the skysail after them. For a beat-up, run-down piece of armor, this exo could really move. We headed south . . . sort of. The exo dipped and dove, cruising low along the Old Awash river, which ran through gullies and ravines to the eastern woredas. Once it even slipped inside the portion of the New Awash river that floated ten meters up in the air, carrying water to Addis Prime and the Gebeya in semi-invisible chutes.

Every so often the stranger would pilot their exo high and just hover, taking stock of where we were, or maybe where our pursuers were. Finally, after a half hour or so of zigzagging, we came to a stop in a shallow valley I'd never seen before. Brown-and-green hills climbed and rolled and dipped all around us, confusing the eye and preventing me from getting a good read on where we were.

When the skysail landed, I took a deep breath. The Ibis slowly let go of the controls and sat back. Besa lay still at my feet, her eyes closed. "Well," I said, my voice threatening to break. "That was fun."

The Ibis glared at me and I tried a smile, but it faded quickly as the stranger's voice echoed through the skysail again. This time I could pay attention, and my jaw dropped. It was coming from Besa's speakers!

"Come, little warriors," the stranger said. "Leave your cat. Disturbing her will only exacerbate her injuries, and I'm afraid I don't have the skill to make repairs. Otherwise I wouldn't be flying around in this beat-up thing. Quickly now! Into the compound."

"What compound?" the Ibis muttered, but she opened the skysail and we hopped out. Bright yellow-and-orange flowers with petals like spikes covered the hill slopes, and the beginnings of a forest grew in the distance.

Besa yowled weakly. I stopped and knelt down, resting my hand on her paw. "Easy, now. Easy. Just rest. I'm going to get help . . . somehow."

I climbed out of the cockpit and started walking after the Ibis, who was moving down the slope when —

— she disappeared!

I stopped and stared after her, confused. The hill dropped, but not that much. Did she fall? I picked my way around a high stand of grass, peeked inside the grass, then moved to the spot I'd last seen her. A valley waited at the bottom, covered in a carpet of blues, greens, and orange-speckled gold. But that was it. I took a step forward, utterly confused. One moment there was nothing but grass and flowers, and the next —

— my face brushed against something,

111

like cloth, and then the image of the valley parted like a curtain. "A workshop?"

The Ibis stood just inside the hidden entrance and whistled. "Adaptive camouflage netting. That stuff's expensive." Sure enough, semitransparent netting rippled in the air above us. Like spiderwebs of starlight, the shimmering material covered the entire slope and was propped up by poles. Below it, stretched down along the rest of the shallow hill and nestled among the flowers, was a beat-up workbench, an old exo repair station that looked like a closet made out of engine parts, and a large tent with the flaps rolled back. I could see a familiar cot inside that made the breath catch in my throat.

It looked like the same sort of cot Uncle Moti kept in his office.

"Well then," the stranger said from right behind me, so close I jumped half a meter into the air.

Suddenly, I became very, *very* aware that we'd followed a perfect stranger into their territory. Uncle Moti's voice rang in my head. *Always know your escape routes. Plan ahead, find the traps.* I kicked myself mentally. Just because we'd escaped one threat didn't mean others didn't exist.

The exo's helmet followed me as I backed up, my mouth moving a mile a minute. "Hey, didn't see you there. Listen, thanks for the assist. You really got us out of a tough spot, but we should go now. Um, send me a bill? I've got the birr to cover it. I just, uhh, need to get it from my other pants. So . . . yes. That's what I have to do. Anyway, it's been fun!"

Besa yowled somewhere behind me. I winced. She needed help, but was this stranger the answer? Sometimes, the enemy of my enemy was just another enemy.

I took another step back and clipped my heel on something, just as I heard the Ibis yell, "Careful!" It was an old warbow with a mechanical quiver attached. It tangled my legs and nearly sent me sprawling to the ground. The stranger's exo shook, and I realized they were laughing. The warbow they were holding dropped, and a hand reached up to the cracked, tinted faceshield. It slid up halfway before it got stuck. The laughter stopped, and muttered curses that would've made Uncle Moti blush came from inside the helmet. I narrowed my eyes. The pilot was a woman, and she *was* speaking Afar! I caught a glimpse of curly white hair and brown eyes. Both her hands gripped the faceshield and tried to force it the rest of the way, while the Ibis and I stood there, confused.

"C'mon, you silly piece of junk! Stop being difficult or I'll sell you to the teff haulers. I . . . said . . . stop being difficult!" Finally, with a shove, the faceshield went up, and I stared into the face of an older, brown-skinned woman. Sweat dripped down her forehead, and she sighed. "Stubborn thing, that is for sure."

The Ibis took a step backward, toward the outside, but the Afar woman shook her head. "I wouldn't do that, little one. The Werari have identified you now. You'll want no part of the captain back there. I tangled with him once, and it's a wonder my exo isn't completely destroyed."

But the Ibis continued to retreat, back to where her skysail waited.

"I said —" the woman began.

"She can't understand you," I interrupted, hoping my Afar wasn't too rusty. The only person I'd ever practiced it with was my uncle Moti during lessons. "But, uh, she thanks you, too. We have to go fix Besa, though. If anything happens to her, I don't know what I'll do. So . . . thank you, um, for getting us out of there, but we really should be . . ."

I paused. The woman was exiting the exo, and when she stepped down, I couldn't help but stare. She was older than I thought. Like, almost Uncle Moti's age. She pulled her bushy white curls back into a bun and secured it with a colorful wrap. She wore an old pilot's jumpsuit and barely came up to my shoulders! But the most surprising thing was when she closed up the now-empty exo and entered a series of commands on the holo-display on its side. The power armor began to rattle and shake. The armor disappeared as its chest plate rotated. The torso widened, the faceshield dropped, and the ends of its arms reconfigured from deadly appendages capable of ripping through a spaceship's hull into a molded pincer that reminded me of a cupholder.

"It's a disguise," I said, astonished.

The reconfigured exo toddled off to the brazier in the corner, steaming all the way. There, it rummaged through supplies, set a pot on the hot coals, and dropped something inside, swirling as it poured.

"Is . . ." I started to say, then paused. "Is the exo making coffee? Wait. It's a bunamech. You disguised your exo as a bunamech." The automated coffee bots were commonly seen along the streets of Addis Prime. You couldn't walk ten meters through a kebele without smelling the aromatic scent of bunamechs roasting their unique blends of coffee beans.

"Not just any coffee, Yared. Highland Arabica — the best."

I shook my head, amazed. It was actually pretty ingenious. Bunamechs went everywhere, including into Authority-restricted complexes. That meant the strange woman could walk inside the most heavily guarded of areas and be the most dangerous person there, without carrying a single weapon on her person.

I turned to her, then paused. She was looking at me . . . almost reverently. Alarm bells went off in my head. "How did you know my name?" I asked slowly.

The woman smiled. "I know a lot about you. I know who's after you, too, and why the Werari won't stop until they capture you . . . or until we defeat them."

Uncle Moti's warnings continued to echo in my head. *Trust no one.* I continued to back up. "The Werari. The fake Authority troops back there? How do I know you're not with them?"

The smile dropped. "Don't be silly, Yared, I just —"

"How do you *know my name?*" I said, my voice nearly a shout.

The exo creaked to a stop, then slowly turned, the coffee forgotten. The woman held out both hands. "Calm, my friend. He's just stressed, that he is. He's not a threat." Somehow, through all the tension, I realized she was talking to the exo, which'd moved closer to the warbow. That was too much.

"Okay, we're leaving. Ibis?"

"About time," she muttered.

From somewhere up the hillside, hidden from sight, I heard my metal lioness yowl. I gritted my teeth. We were wasting time in here while she needed repairs. I backed up, making sure to keep the exo, the warbow, and the pilot in my sight at all times.

"Careful, little warrior," the older woman said, though she didn't try to hinder us. "You don't know what you're dealing with out there. The Werari will not stop. They've seen your face. They've seen where you live, know your history. You don't know what they're capable of. They know your name, Yared."

The Ibis slipped outside the camouflage net and I started to follow, then stopped. I stood there, breathing heavily. The warm air that had carried the aroma of wildflowers inside now felt hot and oppressive. I met the narrowed brown eyes of the pilot, her hands on her hips, and I pointed at her.

"You know my name, too. And sorry to say it, because you seem nice, but I don't know what you're capable of." With that, I backed out of the workshop, just trying to keep my legs from shaking. I held my head high and clenched my fists.

The last thing I saw was the older woman's eyes. Narrowed, yes. Focused, yes. But . . . just as I stepped out of the hidden workshop, I thought I saw her expression change to one of sorrow.

CHAPTER FIVE

I had to fix Besa. Then I had to find Uncle Moti. If I could locate him, he'd explain all of this away. The giant creature, the — what had the lady called them? — the Werari. Every single one of his wild stories had turned up in Addis Prime, and they all wanted a piece of me. And if *they* were real, then . . .

No, that was still too much to think about.

It turned out that I wouldn't have time to wrestle with the as-yet-unthought thoughts about a certain kingdom in the sky, however, because five minutes after zooming away from the hidden workshop in the highlands, the Ibis brought the sky-sail to a sudden stop. I tumbled forward, and Besa landed on top of me.

Did I mention she'd recently grown

mysterious spikes?

Pretty sure I did. And to make matters worse, she was still leaking oil from the damage on her side.

"Why are we stopping?" I squeaked. The lioness yowled an apology and climbed off me. "We need to find a place where I can repair Besa, and then — Hey, don't land! Keep going!"

The Ibis didn't speak as she settled the craft in a small stand of acacia trees in the middle of nowhere. The sun was beginning to set behind the highlands, and I could just make out the Ghebbi peaks in the northeast. Home. Or at least it had been. Now I had nowhere to go. No one waiting for me.

The Ibis turned in her seat and stared, not saying a word, just studying me. I raised an eyebrow, and when she still didn't speak, I glanced at Besa. "Do you know what this is about?" I asked.

"Mrowr."

"Hey, that's not nice. And I took a shower this morning . . . I think."

The Ibis finally let out a slow breath. "Tell me," she said slowly, "why I shouldn't kick you out of my skysail right now."

My jaw dropped open. "I didn't do —"

"Tell me," she continued in an even tone. "Tell me why I should keep helping you. Give me one good reason. Because so far, Yared, all I've heard is a lot of boasting and bragging. A lot of half-truths and even more lies. And yet I'm dragging you all over Addis Prime, risking my *life.*"

I shook my head. "I told you, I don't know what's going on."

The skysail's hatch hissed open, and the Ibis pointed to the grass outside. "Out."

"Ibis —"

"OUT!" Her eyes glittered with rage. I opened my mouth, then shut it.

"Fine," I said. "Come on, Besa." I hopped down from the skysail, disturbing a cloud of gnats as I landed in nearly waist-high grass. I didn't have to explain myself. If she didn't want to help, fine. All I had to do was figure out where I was, walk the . . . hundreds of miles back to Addis Prime and . . . find someplace to stay where the Werari and a three-story monster wouldn't be able to find me.

I paused. *Their* three-story monster. The Bulgu. At least, that's what Uncle Moti had always said when he told his stories. The Werari always controlled the Bulgu. So . . . an evil conquering army and their monster on a leash were looking for me. All I had to do was avoid them, find my uncle, and escape.

Okay, not the easiest of to-do lists, but not impossible. I hoped.

I looked up. "Besa? Let's go."

"Mrowr." The lioness stared at me from the skysail, both paws up on the edge, her tail whipping back and forth in irritation.

"What do you mean I'm being stubborn? She told me to get out; I got out. I can do this by myself."

"Mrowr."

"I am not! Yared the Great is a solo act, anyway, remember? Now come help me with my solo act!"

The tail swished again, and then — with what I swear was a disdainful snarl — the lioness had the nerve to paw at the controls, closing the hatch. *My* lioness! If you can't trust the bionic feline friend you've had since birth, what was the world coming to? Now she was taking sides with my rival!

The two of them glared at me from inside the skysail, and I gritted my teeth. The shadows were growing longer. I had no place to go and no idea what to do next. If I was going to find Uncle Moti, drastic measures had to be taken.

I threw up my hands in disgust. "Fine!"

The hatch hissed open, and the Ibis crossed her arms across her chest. "Talk. Now."

As I climbed back inside, I shook my head at Besa, who was studying her claws with the most . . . well, catlike look of innocence I'd ever seen.

"Traitor," I muttered.

I sat down, and the lioness bumped my knee with her head. I sighed and rubbed her as she settled by my feet again, my fingers tracing the jagged rip along her flank. "You want to know what's going on? Fine. I'll tell you. But don't say I didn't warn you. And can we please go somewhere that has what I'll need to fix Besa?"

The Ibis's gaze dropped to the puddle of oil on the skysail floor, and her eyes softened. She gave a single, terse nod, then sat at the controls. "You talk; I'll fly."

By the time I finished telling Uncle Moti's legend of Axum story, the same one I'd told in Mrs. Marjani's class that morning, the sun had completely set and night had fallen over Addis Prime and its woredas. We'd flown in a large semicircle, avoiding the main city and any place where the Authority or their drones would spot us. A giant, low-hanging cloud bank, silver against the night sky, floated overhead. It blocked out part of the Authority Net, and we flew directly underneath it. The Ibis entered a series of commands. The noise outside the aircraft — the shouts of the night vendors, the buzzing rumbles of construction drones, and even the harsh cries of Besa's archenemy, the undertaker bird — all of it faded away.

She looked at me. "Stealth mode."

"Why —" I started to ask, but then she yanked back on the controls, and we shot up. Higher than I'd ever been before. High enough to attract a lot of unwanted attention from the Authority Net. "Hey, if we get caught, we're all in trouble!"

The skysail sliced upward.

"Um," I said.

We were heading straight up now. The clouds grew larger and larger outside. Ready for the impact of hundreds of stasis turrets firing at us, I closed my eyes —

— only to open them when I heard a familiar, chest-vibrating proximity alarm shake the sky. A massive oval platform had emerged from the clouds, dozens of thrusters firing in rapid succession as it hovered above us. The Ibis sent the skysail up through a large hatch that had appeared on the underside. Darkness surrounded us on all sides as we raced upward, until finally we passed through another opening and entered a sprawling, hilly landscape covered in trees and bushy plants. It was as if we'd emerged into a different world.

"An orbital farm? You took us to an

orbital farm?" I asked, confused.

"Not just any orbital farm," the Ibis said, setting us down in the middle of a large coffee field. It reminded me of the rolling, farm-covered hills of the Oromia region. "This is my family farm. My parents own it. And if they know what I've been up to, we'll both be in huge trouble. So maybe keep your voice down, okay?"

I started to crack a joke, when Besa shifted in my arms. Her metal frame was heavy — really heavy — and her new spikes were jabbing me in my arms and thighs. I didn't care. She was barely moving. I had to fix her. If I lost her, I'd . . .

No, I couldn't think like that.

"I've got you," I whispered.

Her tail flicked, but that was it.

The Ibis looked back at me but didn't say anything. She helped us down, and we walked in silence between the fragrant rows of coffee plants. I think Uncle Moti's story finally convinced her I was losing my grip on reality. Sky cities and burning legions and legendary warriors? I mean, I understood. It was fine. I'd want nothing to do with my problems, either. Again — conquering army and scary monster. So, I got it. As soon as I fixed Besa, we'd go our separate ways and go back to being rivals. Sooner the better.

The orbital farm had two large houses at its center, and just a short walk away was a storage shed and an open-air pavilion. I could hear laughter and music coming from one of the houses. The Ibis kept her head straight, but I couldn't help but try to catch a glimpse of a family being normal. What was that like? Living in the same place that your parents lived in, all of you sharing in the comfort of being close.

I squeezed Besa a little tighter. All I had was my uncle Moti and my Besa. Now I couldn't find one, and the other was —

No. I wasn't going to think like that. Had to keep focused. The houses and the shed were the only structures in the area. We were surrounded by green farmland as far as I could see. Rows and rows of small coffee trees stretched into the distance, separated into plots. Rapid-transit walkways connected them to the compound. A simulated night breeze moved through the farm, circulated by the ventilation system. It rustled the plants and carried an aroma of something bubbling on a stove.

The Ibis led us to the small shed. My throat was raw from spilling everything I knew about the day's events and their connection to Uncle Moti's stories. A blanket of exhaustion settled on me.

"Come on," the Ibis said, and she stepped up to the door. I followed, supporting Besa, then paused at a plant whose bright stalk and pungent flower jogged a memory loose in my head.

"Is this a Sleep-Tree?"

"What? Oh yeah. We grow those here, too. Now where is that lamp . . . ?"

I studied the plant while the Ibis worked. Uncle Moti used to make a tea out of the plant's dried leaves. He said it helped him sleep without dreams, though I think he meant nightmares. I say that because there were nights where I'd wake up and find him leaning over the sink, a haunted expression on his face as he splashed himself with water. Other nights

I don't think he slept at all. When I asked him about it once, he gave me a distracted smile and stared off into the distance.

Sometimes, he'd said, *I don't know what scares me more. The things we did, or the things we chose not to do. I guess history will be the judge.* Then he sent me back to bed as he made himself a pot of tea. I remember thinking there was something reassuring about knowing people who you thought had their lives together and could do what they wanted still needed help sleeping from time to time. It made me feel better about the nights I stared into the darkness, wondering if my parents were still out there, looking for me.

I grabbed a few leaves that had fallen into the hovering pot and held them to my nose. They reminded me of Uncle Moti, so I slipped them into my pocket.

"Yared?"

The Ibis called me. Besa was wriggling and continued to leak oil with every step I took. I needed to get her into a workshop, and fast. But when I saw the logo on the door of the shed, I stumbled to a stop.

"What are we doing?" I whispered.

The Ibis raised an eyebrow. "Fixing your cat. Then we'll figure out what to do next."

"We?"

The Ibis bit her lip, then shrugged. "You might be a jerk sometimes. Rude, loud, and wrong — and not always in that order. And I'm not exactly sure how you — and now me — are wrapped up in this mess. But there's no way you can face flying sword-soldiers and a giant robot monster by yourself. So let's find your uncle, and then you can go back to being that annoying kid I'm always beating."

I opened my mouth, then closed it. I didn't know what to say. To have someone, and my rival at that, stick by me, after years of me and Uncle Moti doing it on our own. Well . . . it felt nice.

She stepped forward and reached for the door handle.

"Whoa," I said, and pointed to the giant A stamped on the door of the storage shed. "Are you sure? This is an Authority symbol."

"Who do you think we buy equipment from? Who do you think gives us the license to fly this close to the Net? That symbol means this will be one of the last places they search. Relax, I come here all the time to tinker with the skysail. No one ever shows up unless there's a problem. Now, come on."

She waved her hand in front of the door and a digital keypad appeared. Her fingers blurred over the surface, and with a soft beep, the door hissed open. I carried Besa inside, then paused, my jaw falling to the floor so fast it broke the sound barrier.

"This . . . this . . ."

The Ibis grinned. "Is awesome?"

The inside of the storage shed was an HKO player's dream setup. Holo-displays lined three of the four walls, each running different scenarios from previous matches. There was the Floodwaters match (I won that one) and the Great Sandstorm (the Ibis barely won that match . . . barely). I didn't even need glasses to see them — they reacted to me as I walked by. In the far corner rested a workbench. I gaped as I carried Besa the last few steps and set her down gently atop it.

"Is that the newest three-turbine nefasi?" I asked. The flightpack gleamed with its ivory-and-silver trim, the shoulder straps smooth.

"Yep," the Ibis said proudly.

I continued to take it all in. She'd turned the shed into a place of comfort. Pictures cycled on a screen in the corner. The Ibis laughing with a group of girls, all of them ranging in age from toddlers to near adults. They shared the same smile, the same eyes. More screens with other pictures floated along the walls. A man and a woman swinging a younger version of the Ibis between them. A sky-sail, brand-new and gleaming. The whole family, lying on their backs on a patch of dirt with a single coffee plant sprouting in the center of them.

"Our first coffee crop that actually made a profit instead of paying off bills," the Ibis said, returning with an armful of oil bulbs and handing me several. She nodded at the lioness on the bench. "Is she going to be okay?"

Besa raised her head briefly, then let it

droop again. The Ibis rubbed her gently between her ears.

"I think so. But I can't reach the leak. I'm going to have to cut around it to get inside. Do you have something —"

She held out a handheld power torch. I bit my lip and took it. My hands were shaking. Sweat pooled on my forehead and ran down my face. The bright orange tip generated lots of heat, but it was the only thing that could cut through diranium metal. Still, if I slipped, or messed up . . .

The Ibis pursed her lips. "Let me take a look." She shot me a glance when I hesitated. "I told you I worked on drones. I can help." I took a deep breath and stepped aside. She got to work, smoothly cutting around the tear in Besa's flank. "Okay, first things first, we have to find the leak and seal it. Does she have a service panel?"

I popped off the damaged flank armor, and we got to work. Besa wriggled as the Ibis siphoned out oil and checked her hydraulics, but I whispered to her, dropping to my knees and maintaining eye contact. The Ibis and I switched off every so often — Besa's components were heavy and it was tiring work. I remember Uncle Moti doing a lot of this when we built her. Where was he now? I could've really used his presence.

We continued to work, one of us making repairs while the other worked to keep Besa calm. Nearly a half hour later, I stepped back and wiped my face, getting grimy oil everywhere. I nodded at the Ibis, and she helped me pop the armor back into place.

"That should do it," I said. "I think we got all the leaks."

The Ibis grinned and held up a greasy hand.

I rolled my eyes but smiled and gave her a high five, splattering oil everywhere. "Why not? Okay Besa, let's check your telemetry."

The virtual keyboard popped out of her back, and a holo-display appeared. I entered in a few commands. "Diagnostics look good; functionality seems normal. Movement . . . hmm."

"What?" the Ibis asked, peering over my shoulder.

I hesitated, then turned the display toward her. "That."

"Looks like a normal set of instructions."

"It is, but it shouldn't be there."

The Ibis shrugged. "So there's something you don't know. Who would've guessed?"

"No, you don't understand. I've been through each and every line of Besa's operating firmware. Just this morning in fact, to prepare for —" I cut myself off before I revealed too much about my HKO preparations. The Ibis smirked. I cleared my throat. "Anyway, it wasn't there this morning. I've never seen this code before. It's . . . it's like it was hidden from me."

"Well," she said, leaning over to study it some more. "What does it do?"

I traced the line of code with my finger, my expression going from annoyed to astonished. "The spikes on her side. It activated them for protection purposes."

"Guardian Protocol," the Ibis read, following my finger. "Sounds impressive. Installed by a General Berihun. You know that person?"

I shook my head, still sort of speechless. Besa had this hidden in her all this time?

"Let's see what it has," the Ibis said. "Upgraded armor. Defensive grid. Enhanced targeting system. Those sound fun. Wait . . . what's that?"

We both leaned in and read it at the same time.

"Homing locator."

I frowned. Homing locator? Did Uncle Moti put this in Besa without telling me? What would he want her to locate? Me? But Besa was always by my side. Maybe . . .

My eyes widened and excitement coursed through me. My fingers flew over the keyboard. The Ibis gawked. "What are you doing? You don't know what —"

"I think this can help me find Uncle Moti!" I said.

"You don't know that!"

EXECUTE? the display blinked. I ignored the Ibis and stabbed at the keyboard —

— and a map made of brilliant silver light swirled inside the room, with Besa at its center.

The bionic lioness raised her head, letting out a massive roar that rattled the walls of the small shed. The Ibis and I backed up, speechless. The different woredas of Addis Prime swirled around her, filling up the room until we were standing in a three-dimensional miniature city. She stood and shook herself, acting like she'd never been injured, then hopped down from the workbench. The map continued to sharpen into valleys, forests, and a city that I recognized.

Along with a fortress on top of a mountain that I didn't.

"That's Addis Prime," the Ibis said, staring at the city. But I couldn't focus on that.

"Besa?" I whispered.

The lioness . . . my lioness turned to look at me. Silver words blinked into existence above the map, bright and searing, as if trying to burn their way into my subconscious.

GUARDIAN PROTOCOL ACTIVATED.

CHAPTER SIX

We stared at each other, brown eyes meeting silver eyes.

The map. Was that what the fake Authority troops — the ones the old pilot had called the Werari — were after? Or was it something else? And when did someone program it, anyway? I'd had Besa for as long as I could remember. Uncle Moti had said we'd been together my whole life.

Uncle Moti. I still needed to find him. Was he supposed to be somewhere on the map? Maybe he'd have the answers. If we could just get a moment to breathe and make a plan. I shifted in my seat, and Besa cocked her head. Her eyes never left my own as she prowled to the left, then the right, the map moving with her. Just as I began to move to her, a blinking gold icon in the shape of a lion cub appeared in the center of the holographic map . . . then floated to hover directly in front of my face, words appearing just above it.

ESTABLISHING LINK.

The lion cub stretched and bounded toward me playfully. It paced in a circle and shook its tiny mane. It opened its mouth to let out a silent roar.

Then it began to transform, briefly morphing into a replica of my face. My jaw dropped — and so did the replica's. I closed my mouth, and it did the same. I made a face and —

"Can you be serious for one second? A single second?" the Ibis asked.

The replica dissolved back into a lion cub.

"Whoa," I whispered.

LINK ESTABLISHED. ANALYZING THREATS . . .

Besa swiveled her head to look at the Ibis.

She held up her hands. "Hey, Besa, it's me, remember?"

I held my breath as Besa prowled over, sniffed at the Ibis's hands, then returned to stand in front of me. The golden lion cub bounded away, returning to the map. It bobbed in the air above the Oromia hills, outside Addis Prime. Then a new shape appeared, a large, flattened oval that floated in the sky.

"That's our orbital," the Ibis whispered.

The floating farm hovered above the ground. Besa let out a low growl. Before I could try to calm her down, a small section of the map blinked red. Her head swung to the door, the growl growing in strength as it rumbled through the shed.

THREATS INCOMING, ONE THOUSAND METERS AND CLOSING.

Red dots appeared on the map. Six or seven, arranged in a wide semicircle, sweeping toward the lion cub icon from all directions. Right toward the orbital farm.

"Is that because of us?" the Ibis asked, terror written all over her face. She took a half step backward. "Are they coming for *us*?"

EIGHT HUNDRED METERS AND

CLOSING.

"The Werari." I didn't know why I was so positive, but the overwhelming sense of danger told me we didn't have time to waste. "We have to go," I said. "Now. Ibis. Ibis! The skysail, let's go!"

"But the farm. My family! We can't just leave them here!"

I groaned. She was right. Besides, it wasn't like they were after her. I just had to escape, and maybe the Werari would leave her alone. "Fine. If they come here, though, tell them the truth. I made you bring me here to repair Besa. Maybe they'll leave you alone. Come on, Besa."

We sprinted to the door and ran outside. The hologram faded from view as Besa led the way, but I nearly tripped over her as she skidded to a stop and snarled. Pinpricks of light flashed through the transparent bubble shield arching over the farm. At first I thought they were stars or a glitching section of the Authority Net. But then the pinpricks began to grow, and the realization of what I was looking at sent chills down my spine.

"The Werari. Besa, we need to go, and now."

She yowled in agreement. We started to run, but a shout stopped us.

"Hey!" It was the Ibis. "What are you going to do, jump off the orbital and pretend to be rain? Get in!" She climbed into the skysail, and then, seconds later, the two of us followed her.

"Thank you," I said.

"Yeah, yeah. If you get caught, those goons are going to talk to my parents, and they might get in trouble. So you'd better not get caught."

"Yes, ma'am!" I shouted.

She punched me lightly, then powered up the skysail. Within seconds, we were airborne, shooting back down through the maintenance hatch and speeding away from the orbital farm and into the night sky.

"Where to?" the Ibis asked. "I'm all out of hiding spots, and they know where you live."

Besa stiffened.

SEVEN HUNDRED METERS AND CLOSING.

The Ibis said something rude under her

breath that made my eyes widen. "They're too fast," she said. "We need to lose them."

I looked out the hatch window at the ground below us. It was all farmland. More coffee fields and mobile hydroponics units. High above us, other bubble-shaped orbital teff farms rotated gently. They would've been good places to lie low, but they belonged to different families, and we had no way of sneaking aboard.

No, we needed someplace where it was easy to get lost in the crowds, with plenty of entrances and exits so we wouldn't get trapped. Someplace like . . .

I inhaled sharply and turned to the Ibis. "I know where to go."

SIX HUNDRED METERS AND CLOSING.

I pointed to the large shadowy sphere hovering on the horizon, its giant thrusters still sputtering but somehow managing to hold steady.

"The Gebeya."

"You have got to be joking," the Ibis said. But even as she spoke, the neon controls reengaged around her hands and her fingers flew across the display. She spoke low and urgently as she increased our speed. "Why would we go *back* there? That's where this all started."

I nodded. "Exactly. They've already searched there. No one will ever think to check the market twice. We can get lost in the alleys, hang out there for a few hours to make sure no one is tracking us, and then, bam — off we go on our separate ways. Now that I have the map I can keep an eye out for the Werari while I find Uncle Moti."

"The map."

"Yep."

"The one that was buried in the firmware of your bionic lioness. The one you had no idea existed five minutes ago. That map?"

I grinned. "What do you have against maps?"

The Ibis shot me a look, but she leaned

into the controls and pushed the throttle forward, coaxing every bit of speed out of the skysail she possibly could. After a moment, she inhaled and exhaled slowly. "Fine. Maybe those . . . people —"

"The Werari."

"Yeah, them. Maybe they'll leave my family alone, now that we're gone. Maybe I can sneak into my room later, and no one will have noticed I never came home. Everything can go back to normal."

"See? My plan is foolproof."

"Says the fool." The Ibis tried to smile, but her face crumpled into a worried frown as she glanced behind us. The Werari still kept pace. She continued to pour on speed as she muttered, "We've got to lose them. Hang on."

"Why do I need to —" I started to say, before the skysail dipped suddenly down and tilted left. We shot into a ravine, skimmed along the remnants of a stream, then plunged into a field of golden-colored grass. The high stalks formed a canopy as the Ibis piloted, likely unable to see two meters in front of us. She studied the skysail's display, then jerked the ship to the right.

"Whoops!" she said.

" 'Whoops'? 'Whoops'?! Do you even know what you're doing? Where are we —"

But again my words were cut off as we zipped out of the grass and raced toward the outskirts of a residential woreda. One- and two-story homes, cube-shaped as most of the colony's habitats were, stretched out from left to right. The narrow streets and even narrower alleyways were empty, save for one or two hovercans making the rounds, puttering through the shadows.

Behind us, I could count six Werari exos still doggedly pursuing us. They shadowed our every move like homing missiles. "Can you lose them in the alleys?" I called out.

"I'm going to try."

The skysail swept around a hovercan and dashed into an alley. It was a tight fit, and I winced once or twice as we barely missed clipping a corner or a wall. A left turn. A right. Another left. Across a street and into another alley. Each maneuver sent my stomach lurching, but as I watched, the Werari grew farther and

148

farther from our tail, until finally I didn't see them at all.

Was that it? Had we lost them? "We're clear," I said. "We can head to the market."

"Are you sure?"

"I think so." I turned around and draped an arm over Besa, careful to avoid her spikes. The Ibis took us through one more alley, then aimed the skysail at the Gebeya, visible on the horizon even now. The stars in the sky were few and faint, but there was still enough light to see the damage done. Whole sections of the floating market had been crumpled, and long furrows had been raked along the underside. I shivered as I remembered the claws of the bionic monster ripping stalls and panels apart to reach me.

The Ibis bit her fingernails, one by one, until finally she let her hands drop and turned to face me.

"Uh . . ." I said, pointing to the controls, "shouldn't you be, you know, flying?"

"I need to know my family is going to be safe," she said. "Those people . . . that thing . . . they're not going to hurt my mother and father, or my sisters, right? Tell me they aren't. Tell me they'll be safe."

I started to thump my chest, but she whipped her head back and forth so fast the skysail rocked in midair. My eyes shot to the Gebeya, growing steadily closer. The Ibis grabbed my shoulder.

"No, don't do that. Don't flex. Don't brag. Don't lie to me." She took a deep breath. "That coffee farm has been in my family for generations. My great-great-grandparents planted those rows. My grandfather built the first orbital by hand. If they get in trouble . . ."

Her voice trailed off. I sat there, one hand on Besa, the other clenched in my lap. I got it. No really, I did. Family is everything. Uncle Moti said it all the time: Family powered us, be it the ones we were born with or the ones we found. I never understood how you could find family, but I guess that was something you figured out as an adult.

The Ibis was worried about her family. I was worried about Uncle Moti. I knew how the fear of something happening to them could wiggle its way into your bones and lock them in place, until it felt like all the blood in your veins had been replaced by fear.

I rapped my knuckles on Besa's flank, the metallic sound filling the skysail, and put as much confidence into my voice as possible. "Nothing will happen to your family . . . I promise. They're looking for a kid and his lion. That's it. They're following —"

I stopped.

"Yared?" the Ibis asked. "That wasn't too reassuring. Are you okay?"

"They're following me," I said slowly. "How? How did the Werari find me? That monster, it was staring straight at me in the Gebeya. Then they found us at your family farm. How?"

We stared at each other, then looked at Besa. My lioness licked her paw, then froze as she realized we were studying her.

"Rowr?"

"Can they track the Guardian Protocol?" I asked.

The Ibis shook her head. "That wasn't

activated when the monster attacked, remember?"

"Right."

Besa backed up as far as she could go. "Rowr?"

"Shh," I said, "this won't hurt. I just have to . . . turn you inside out. Easy."

But as I reached for her panel, an alarm started blaring inside the skysail. The Ibis whirled around and grabbed the controls, swerving to avoid several clothing stalls at the last moment. We ducked through a main artery of the market, normally filled to the brim with people shopping for supper. Now it was wide and empty. We'd arrived at the Gebeya.

And we weren't alone.

"Welcome back" came a harsh, filtered voice.

Floating in the middle of the wide, empty aisle was a familiar battered exo. Blue-white flames jetted out of its thrusters. It held a long spear in one hand, with a tip of flickering silver plasma that filled the area with a harsh glow. The spear raised to point at me.

"Come with me. Now."

■ ■ ■ ■

The tip of the lightspear rippled, then disappeared as the plasma weapon shut off. The exo floated down to the floor, landing with a thump in the aisle, between the remains of a fruit vendor and a nearly intact butcher stall. More debris tumbled down, and dust clouds billowed back into the darkness. The thrusters fell silent, their blue-white glow fading away, and the narrow passage fell into gloom.

Speakers crackled on the exo. "You are running out of time, little ones."

Why does every grown-up take that same familiar tone of voice? The one that makes it seem like you wouldn't be in whatever problem you're currently entangled in if you'd just listened to them? Was it just me? Was I the only one who noticed that? I started to ask a question, but the Ibis shifted and grabbed the skysail's controls.

"Go to the Gebeya," she muttered. "We can hide out there. Great plan."

"What are you doing?" I asked as she pressed several buttons.

"Going to cloak and getting out of here. What do you think I'm doing?" She pressed a few more switches, then slowly began to ease the skysail back the way we came. "Get ready. We're out of here in three . . . two . . . one . . ."

Alarms blared, and we both flinched.

"What's that?" I yelled.

"I don't know! Everything's normal. It's not me!"

"Rowr!"

We turned to Besa and stopped, horrified. The alerts came from her! The map bloomed from her chestplate without warning. Red icons were rapidly approaching our position, twice as many this time. The Werari had found us, and they were blocking our exit. We were trapped.

"What do we do?" the Ibis asked.

I shook my head, words failing me. The dots moved closer, in neat rows, and I could imagine the footsteps of the impostor soldiers as they marched, shotels out. Or maybe they piloted exos, floating in perfect unison in the gleaming gray powered armor, like flying silverbacks.

"Yared?"

I stared at the Ibis. Her hands gripped the skysail's controls, ready to punch it in any direction that would let us escape. Except there wasn't an escape. The Werari swept toward us from behind, while in front of us . . .

The strange woman in the battered exo twirled her lightspear. "Are you coming, child?" She took a step forward, and her faceshield slid part of the way up, then got stuck. A familiar stream of complaints followed.

"Follow her," I said. The words slipped out of my mouth, as if they'd spoken themselves.

The Ibis gawked. "What?"

"It's her or the Werari. I know which I'd rather choose."

The Ibis made a face, but Besa yowled. The Werari were nearly on top of our position. I could see the dust falling from the ceiling as their footsteps approached. The skysail shot forward, and the Ibis grumbled. "I hope you know what you're doing."

The exo pilot led us inside the butcher's

stall, sidestepped a counter lined with fryers. Steam escaped from one as a batch of shekla tibs sizzled inside. Which was weird, since half the market was damaged and the other half had been abandoned by shoppers and vendors alike. Still, we headed to the back. The old woman swept aside floating pods containing different cuts of beef and lamb, then pressed a button. To my surprise, the whole back wall swung inward, revealing a tunnel wide enough for the skysail to fly through. The pilot pointed with the shaft of the light-spear, the weapon still powered off.

"In here. Quickly. Power your ship down and wait. I'll distract them."

"How?" I called as the Ibis sent the sky-sail into the darkness.

The pilot smiled. Her exo's chestplate split open, and the small woman, still wearing her pilot's jumpsuit, stepped down. She flipped a lever, and the exo twisted in on itself, reconfiguring its shape until it became . . .

"The bunamech," I said, my words almost a whisper.

The service bot from before, the one

that had performed the coffee ritual, now stood in front of us. I shook my head. It was a disguise, and a good one at that. But before I could say so, the old pilot shooed us on.

"Quiet now, or we're all finished. And quickly, take this off." She reached out and tapped the medallion dangling around my neck. "Slip it into the expansion slot in your lioness, young man. It will garble her signal."

I grabbed the medallion, staring at her suspiciously. "Expansion slot?" I asked.

"Behind her right ear. Press it forward and then twist. Now move it!"

I shook my head, hurrying forward. What sort of nonsense was she — Wait . . . she was right! I pushed Besa's ear forward, revealing a small receptacle that I'd never seen before. I stared at it, then slid my medallion into place. Too many questions, not enough time to search for answers.

The woman pushed the wall shut. Darkness fell over us, and I could hear the wall disguised with rubble being shifted back in place. The Ibis and I looked at each other in the dim light, then hopped out of the skysail. We scrambled to a crack in the trapdoor and pressed our eyes to it. The old pilot crouched in the center of the mess, her shoulders slumped and her hair disheveled as she lifted a shattered pod up to the flickering light. The bunamech stood motionless against the opposite wall.

Footsteps approached.

The Werari marched into the small stall. Six of them, with more in the hallway behind them. They spread into a semicircle, surrounding the pilot. No one moved for several seconds. Then their ranks shifted, and a man stepped into the dim light. Golden Eyes. He clasped his hands behind his back. I couldn't avoid staring at the shotel on his waist.

He surveyed the room, sharp eyes missing nothing. They lingered on the bunamech, then returned to the pilot, whose shoulders were shaking. She . . . she was crying?

"My shop, my shop," she said in between sobs, looking up at the soldiers. "What am I going to do?"

Golden Eyes ignored her and glanced at a familiar-looking soldier. The trooper stepped forward and saluted. "The signal was lost in here, sir."

He nodded and motioned a hand forward. "Bring the scanling. Search the shop." His voice was smooth and almost melodic, at total odds with his expression and the blade on his hip. I'd seen what he could do, though.

The soldier stepped forward, wearing a bulky backpack. Now I definitely knew I recognized her from before. She'd been in the market earlier. What was that thing on her back? She squatted with a grunt, and the lid of the backpack unfolded. *Something* emerged. Long silver legs that ended in sharp points. A carapace-like shell. Three orbs glowing a sickly green color had been mounted on top, and they began to spin, sending light bouncing across the room as they whirred faster and faster. The creature — the scanling — looked like a spider and moved like one, too. It scuttled across the butcher shop, pausing here and there as it swept the room.

"Yared," the Ibis whispered. She'd stepped back into the passageway, staring at the darkness behind us.

"We'll be fine," I lied as the scanling drew closer.

It stopped by the back wall, scurried forward a few steps, then stopped again. It backed up. I held my breath. It was mere inches away. If I reached my hand through the gap near the floor I could probably touch it. It was so close I could hear the orbs as they spun, and the *tik tik tik* of its metal legs as it scuttled in place.

"Yared," the Ibis whispered.

The scanling turned toward the hiding place.

Suddenly, the pilot stood up, kicking the pile of pods she'd made and sending them scattering noisily around the room. "Look at my shop!" she screamed at the soldiers. "What am I supposed to do now? Who will buy meat covered in dust and metal? I paid the fees for the herding license with my last savings, and now my shop is ruined. Ruined!" She collapsed once more, sobbing.

It was pretty impressive! I thought I was a good liar, but she wasn't half bad. A herding license cost thousands of birr. If the orbital farms, like the one the Ibis lived on, had a dozen hoops to jump through in order to get the proper license, these were even more of a hassle. You could spend years waiting to get a chance to lease one of the giant platforms where herders raised cattle, goats, and other livestock. Those orbital grazing fields were tough to get a spot on, and the waiting list was probably miles long.

Even more impressive, the disturbance had drawn the scanling's attention. The bionic spider turned, and that's when its orbs registered the bunamech. The scanling stood ramrod-straight, then scuttled across the room in a blur. The orbs froze, their light outlining the disguised exo. I inhaled.

"I think someone's here," the Ibis hissed. I looked at her, ready to ask what she meant, when one of the soldiers spoke hesitantly, drawing my attention back to the scene.

"Sir?"

Golden Eyes was eyeing the woman as he moved toward the bunamech. When he was no more than a meter away, the bunamech came to life. Rattling sounds came from inside its chest plate, and it pulled out a self-heating pan and swirled it, steam already wafting up as its other arm pulled a jebena out of the thin air, as if by magic.

"Selam, sir! Sit and enjoy three cups of coffee." The bunamech took a step forward. The scanling scuttled around it, quivering so hard I thought its legs would fall off. The soldier who'd released it chased after it, apologizing to Golden Eyes.

"Sorry, Captain Ascar. The silly coffee automat must've caught the scanners. I'll recalibrate to ignore it in the future."

Golden Eyes — no, Captain Ascar . . . my pursuer had a name now — glared at the bunamech. Then he transferred his ire to the pilot. He stood in front of her, his angry expression causing even his soldiers to wince. Maybe they'd been on the receiving end of his temper before. Finally, he turned and strode smoothly toward the entrance. There he paused, glaring back into the room.

"Seal the automat and this . . . woman . . . in." With that command, he exited the stall.

The pilot pounded the floor, sobbing and screaming. "No! Please, sir, you can't! My family. My children! Pleeease!"

But the soldiers turned and left as well, the last one gathering the scanling and reattaching it to her back. She pulled out her shotel, the glimmering blade illuminating the stall. With a look of regret — but not a word of apology — she sliced through the door and the struts on either side. The already-unstable walls and ceiling began to shudder, and the pilot continued to scream.

"NO! NOOOO!"

CRASH.

Something fell across the slit in the wall, blocking my view. I couldn't hear anything on the other side. No movement. No cries. Nothing. I stood, horrified, unsure of what to do next. So when the Ibis grabbed my elbow and jerked me backward, I almost shouted in surprise. I would have, except she clamped a hand over my mouth.

"Be quiet!" she hissed. I started to struggle, but she pointed into the darkness behind the skysail. A small glowing light bobbed toward us. "We aren't the only ones in this tunnel!"

The light grew closer and closer. The

Ibis dropped into a defensive crouch, hands extended like knives in front of her. Me? I tried to hide behind Besa, except . . .

"Where's Besa?" I asked, my heart skipping a beat. My lioness wasn't at my side, nor anywhere in the darkness as far as I could see. (Which wasn't far. It was *very* dark.) Where'd she go? Had the soldiers taken her? Was she damaged in the rubble outside? "Besa!"

"Shhh!" The Ibis grabbed my arm. I hadn't realized I'd started moving forward.

"Oh, that's quite all right," a familiar voice said. The light stopped. It grew brighter, until I could see the grizzled face of a man holding up an old-fashioned lantern. Besa stood beside him, and I realized that the man was leaning on her. One of his legs had been wrapped in an air cast. He smiled — a crooked, familiar smile that made my heart lurch in my chest as a wave of relief swept over me. "The soldiers are gone. Not that this fool of a boy would think about that."

It was Uncle Moti.

Audio Transcript File No. 2132.070
Location: [UNDISCLOSED DE-
TENTION FACILITY]
Time: 02:55
Subject: Yared [LAST NAME RE-
DACTED FOR SECURITY]

Auditor: Ah, now we get to the crux
of the matter.

Me: The what, now?

Auditor: Let's talk about this "Uncle
Moti" of yours, shall we?

Me: Well, that's what I was doing
before you interrupted —

Auditor: How much do you know
about the man who raised you? About
his background, his hobbies, his rise
to fame . . . and infamy?

Me: See, I don't like what you just
did there. That little pause you did.
"And infamy . . ." What was that
about?

Auditor: I know about his life before
you. I've seen the records. I've
watched the holovids. And yet there's
so much about him that's still hid-

165

den. Classified, you might say. But what I did find was extremely interesting.

Me: Well, good, maybe you can tell this part of the story, then. I'm tired of talking. Never got my tea with honey, and my stomach's gurgling. You've got something in your nose, you know . . .

Auditor: There's nothing in my nose!

Me: Are you sure? It looks like something hairy is climbing out of it.

Auditor: Something hairy . . . that's my mustache, you [**transcript edited**].

Me: Hey, now, no need for name-calling. You know what? How about I just continue with my story and you can groom your . . . mustache, if that's what you call it?

[faint yowls]

Auditor: Now, then. Maybe this will encourage you to stay on task.

Me: . . .

Me: Is . . . is that a holovid of Besa?

What is that machine? What are you doing?

Auditor: Have you ever seen metal ore heated past its melting point? If you know what's best for you and that tin mouse-catcher, you'll start talking. Trust me . . . the way circuitry bubbles is so disturbing. So, once more . . . I'd like to hear more of the *infamous* Moti's life since taking you in, and why he's suddenly reappeared after so many years —

Me: . . .

Auditor: . . .

Me: . . . Fine . . . what do you want to know?

Auditor: Simple. Why did you decide to betray him?

CHAPTER SEVEN

"You're alive."

The two words rattled around inside my head, growing and growing in volume until they were the only ones I could think to say. My uncle. Alive. Hurt, but alive — and not in the hands of those Werari troopers. I took a step forward, then another, and then suddenly we were hugging. Uncle Moti's arms crushed me as he rubbed my hair and held me. "Never a doubt, my boy," he whispered. "Never a doubt."

I pushed him away and shook my head. The relief disappeared, quickly replaced by a growing anger. The day's events — from learning about my uncle begging for money, to realizing that the stories he'd told me for years weren't stories, but reality — everything boiled up inside me until I felt like I would burst with frustration. What else hadn't he told me? Did I have to comb through my entire childhood to determine the truth from the lies?

I pushed him again. "You're alive! The Werari were at our place, and they were the same ones from the marketplace with that . . . that weird bionic monster, and you weren't answering your screen, and I didn't know if you were dead or injured or what and you're alive and I was worried. I was worried!"

I pushed him again, and Uncle Moti grabbed my arms and pulled me into another fierce hug. He didn't say anything; he just hugged me, letting me vent my anger and fear. When I finally fell silent, he took a step back and placed his hands on my shoulders. We stared at each other. Uncle Moti wore a faded jumpsuit, and in the dim light, I could just make out a square area on his chest that wasn't quite as dingy as the rest of the suit. It looked as if something had been removed, and recently. It was the same style of jumpsuit that the pilot woman wore.

The pilot!

Uncle Moti saw the expression on my face and nodded, then tried to smile. "I'll explain everything, I promise. But we're not clear just yet. Quickly now, help me with the door. You too, young lady," he said, speaking to the Ibis.

It was then that I heard the soft but insistent rapping coming from the wall. The three of us grabbed the edges of the hidden door and pulled. It resisted at first, but after a few seconds, the wall groaned and opened, sending dust and small bits of debris raining down on our heads. We stepped back, and the exo pilot stumbled inside in a fit of coughing. Grime smudged her cheeks. The old bunamech followed. I couldn't tell if it was damaged or not, because it was already battered and beat-up. Maybe it had a few more dents? To be honest, it looked better than ever.

Together, Uncle Moti and the pilot shut the hidden door, and she slid a bar into place. "You can never be too sure," she said, speaking in Amharic so the Ibis could understand. She took the lantern from my uncle and linked arms with the astonished girl. "Help me, would you, child? My knee isn't what it used to be. Leave the aircraft, it will be safe here. Now come, everyone. I'll make sambusas, and I think I have a little bit of tej sealed up somewhere. We will share a meal and a story. I think everyone has some explaining to do, yes?"

She turned to me. "Lead the way, Yared."

"Me? I don't know where I'm going."

"Oh?" She raised an eyebrow, then nodded at Besa. "Perhaps you should work with your Guardian."

"My what?"

"Kamali," Uncle Moti said, his voice low in warning. But the pilot — Kamali — flapped a hand at him without turning around.

"He must learn, General, and soon. His ignorance places us all in danger."

I bristled in anger. "I'm not ignorant. And Besa isn't a guard, or whatever you called her. She's my friend. Uncle Moti helped me build her when I was little, right, Uncle . . . ?" But my voice trailed off as I saw the expression on my uncle's face. Sorrow and regret filled his eyes. He dropped to one knee, grunting in pain, and placed one hand on my shoulder. His eyes begged me to understand something I hadn't quite figured out yet. He took a deep breath and held it, as if afraid of releasing the words that would follow.

"He has to learn, General," Kamali repeated.

General? Why does she keep calling him General?

Uncle Moti exhaled, then nodded. "Fine. Back in the Den." He dropped his hand to Besa, who stood beside me. He stared into her eyes and spoke.

"Guardian Protocol, engage Defender mode. Authorization, General Moti Berihun, commander of the Burning Legion of Axum."

Defender mode? That sounded scary. And as he spoke, the room seemed to shrink. No. Besa was growing! The words Uncle Moti had spoken faded as I watched the lioness transform into something . . . greater. Her flanks expanded, the ridge of spikes emerged farther, and a visor-like headpiece unfolded from a hidden gap in her neck, settling over her eyes. She had a menacing appearance.

When her transformation finished, she shook herself.

"Besa?" I whispered.

A low growl rumbled in her throat. I swallowed, extending my hand. She stared at it for a long heartbeat, and then she nuzzled it. I exhaled. She seemed just as confused by what was happening as I was. Behind me, the Ibis gasped. When I glanced back, she was staring at Uncle Moti.

"So it *was* you," she said slowly. "You put the hidden code in Besa's firmware."

That's right. The man who left the hidden instructions. That was my uncle. But I'd never heard him use the surname Berihun before in my life. What happened to Heywat? Did he change his name again? What was going on?

Uncle Moti nodded, a fleeting smile crossing his face before the haunted expression returned. "I had intended to reveal the code to Yared when the time was right. It appears that time is right *now.*"

"And it's quickly running out," Kamali, the pilot, reminded us. She tapped one foot impatiently, then winced and rubbed her knee. "Quickly, child, the Guardian."

My uncle hesitated, then nodded at me. "Go ahead, Yared. Only you or your blood relatives can command Besa now. Even then, they may only do so in dire emergencies." He glanced at Kamali, and they shared some unspoken communication before he spoke again. "In *some* circumstances, she can be commanded to bond with another, temporarily. But she is *your* protector and your guide. So many secrets, so many explanations, so little time."

Genuine frustration crumpled his face, and he let out a giant sigh. For a brief moment, he looked . . . ashamed. As if he wanted to ask for forgiveness but couldn't. Again, he was holding something back. I wanted to grab him, shake him, shout at him — to force him to tell me something, anything! If the Ibis and Kamali weren't here, maybe I would have. Each time I learned something new that he'd kept secret, it was like ripping open a scar I never knew I had. Death by a thousand secrets.

Uncle Moti continued. "Enough of my whining. Have Besa lead us to the Gebeya's Lion Den."

I repeated the instructions, then stopped. Something he'd just said jerked me to a complete halt. When I met his eyes, Uncle Moti's shoulders slumped. Like he'd expected this.

I knew. I *knew!* But I needed to hear him say it. No matter how much it hurt.

"You said only me or my blood relatives could command Besa," I muttered. "But . . . you're my uncle. That's family, right? You're my blood relative."

He looked away.

"You *are* my uncle," I said again desperately. "Aren't you?"

The Ibis looked at me strangely. "Yared? Did you get hit on the head back there? You're not making any sense."

The whole world was crashing down on me. It was like the attack on the Gebeya all over again, except instead of a giant monster upending the markets, it was a collection of words that together formed a revelation too searing hot to look at. A tear prickled at the corner of my eye.

"Who are you?" I asked.

Uncle Moti stood, grimacing as he favored his right leg. He took a deep breath and clasped both hands behind his back. It took me a moment to realize he was standing at attention. Like the soldiers of the Werari behaved with their golden-eyed Captain Ascar. Like a subordinate did to a commanding officer. But what was higher than a general?

"My name is Moti Berihun, and I am a son, mourner, and general of Axum. I have pledged to protect you, Yared — with my life if necessary. I will do so without fail." His words were filled with pride. He *looked* like the same man who'd showed me how to cook injera without making too much of a mess, the man who'd bandaged my injuries after my nefasi malfunctioned. But all those memories faded when his eyes dropped to mine and he spoke his next seven words.

"And . . . no. I am not your uncle."

■ ■ ■ ■

The words sliced through me like the razor-thin edge of a shotel blade.

I am not your uncle.

We walked in silence. The hidden tunnel led deep into the center of the Gebeya, twisting and turning and sometimes ending abruptly. If not for the bright silver outline Besa projected, we would have been completely lost. But we moved, slowly but surely. Everyone kept their thoughts to themselves. I tried to keep my focus on placing one foot after the other, a hand on Besa's back, carefully avoiding the new spikes quivering out of her back. Another transformation I had to get used to.

I am not your uncle.

I'd found Uncle Moti, but now he wasn't my uncle. He was some general of Axum. Which was real, apparently.

I am not your uncle.

"This reminds me of the Gondar campaign."

The Ibis's whisper cut through my thoughts, and I frowned. "What?"

"The Gondar campaign. A few seasons ago in the HKO, remember? Down in the irrigation canals?"

I blinked. We were approaching the end of a narrow hallway. A wide door with several rusty locks securing it appeared out of the gray darkness. I stopped, then shook my head as my mind caught up with what she was saying. The Gondar campaign was a short but popular series of tournaments that unfolded over the course of several weeks. It was one of the first HKO events I ever played in after Uncle Moti . . . I mean, after the man *calling himself* Uncle Moti and I moved here. We'd just left our previous home, outside a small woreda in the Gambela region, southwest of Addis Prime. The players all raced to find Kaleb's Obelisk in the shallow canals that ran beneath the city; the ones that fed the landing pads where the orbital farms and grazing platforms replenished their stores. The HKO competitors all used makeshift boats and tried not to get our glasses wet. It was the first tournament I won, and my first taste of fame. After that, I knew it was my destiny to be the best.

Destiny.

Funny, that word sounded different after today. After the Guardian Protocol and *General* Moti's revelations. In fact, it had been his teachings that helped me win the Gondar campaign. Near the end of the match, after navigating the canals and collecting tokens, I blocked a key intersection with a bunch of buoys and some small boats I later learned were called skiffs. It forced the other players to divert back into the path of the . . .

My hand froze in place on top of Besa's head, and I stopped in my tracks.

No. No way.

"Yared?" Kamali called from the rear of the group, where she leaned on the bunamech for assistance. "Is everything all right? We're almost there."

It couldn't be.

I turned around, and my eyes found Uncle Moti. He held up the lantern. "Yared? What's the matter?"

"Was everything a lie?" I asked, though I don't know if the question was for him or for me. My voice was soft in the dim light, but it still echoed.

"What?"

"The HKO." I looked at the Ibis. "What's the name of the ring we have to stay inside of each round?"

"What does that have to do —"

"Just . . . please. I will explain. Or someone will."

The Ibis rolled her eyes. "You know what it's called. It's called the . . ." Her voice trailed off as she thought, and suddenly, her face grew tight. I knew she'd just made the connection between the day's events and the game every kid in Addis Prime played. "It's called the Invasion."

I nodded and forced myself to turn back to Uncle Moti, while still talking to her. "Do you know what that translates to in Old Amharic? The Werari."

Uncle Moti stepped past me. He produced a key and proceeded to open each lock, catching them before they could land noisily on the ground, and slipped them into one of the many pockets hidden in the folds of his robe. The door opened silently, and he walked inside.

Anger flared inside me.

"No," I said, following him. "You don't get to do that."

"Do what?" he asked absentmindedly, preoccupied with lighting more old lanterns and pulling dust tarps off various crates and piles of equipment.

"Pretend that everything is normal."

"Nothing is ever normal, Yared. Not for us. You have to adapt and think ever forward. To remain in place is to fall behind."

"There it is again!" I exploded. "That's the tagline for the HKO. *Stay in place and you'll fall behind.* Did you know that? Is that why you didn't care if I played the game?"

"Who," he said in between grunts as he reached behind a large, rectangular object, "do you think helped design the game?"

My jaw dropped. In the following silence, Uncle Moti straightened and flipped a switch on a console in the center of the room. More lights came on, modern ones this time. The room was larger than I'd originally thought. It was shallow, but it stretched dozens of meters to the left and right. Portable bunks had been shoved against the wall. A solar generator hummed quietly on the far side, next to a folding table and several stools. It powered a refrigerator, several braziers, and an impressive array of screens. As he powered each one on, different maps appeared, some as radar, some showing topography, and others showing —

"Is that the Gebeya?" the Ibis asked.

I followed her pointing finger. Sure enough, one of the larger screens showed several different views of the damaged floating market. Kamali walked up, tapped in a series of commands. The screen split into thirds, then into thirds again, until nine different feeds appeared. She studied them, then sighed and pointed to one in the top left corner. "They're leaving."

We all watched as Captain Ascar and his Werari troops boarded transport shuttles near the docking pads on the upper levels of the Gebeya. When they took off, Uncle Moti limped to a screen several paces to the left and studied it. It was a map of Addis Prime, and several red dots were speeding to the southeast. Soon, they were off the screen completely.

"They'll be back," he said grimly. "We need to act fast."

"What you need to do," I said, "is tell me the truth. All of it!"

"Watch your tone," he said, turning a sharp look on me.

I folded my arms. "You're not my uncle, remember? Why should I?"

"Yared," he warned.

"Tone! You want to talk about tone? What about the truth? Or honesty? What about lying to me for all these years, feeding me stories and legends, pretending to care about me, when all this time you were living a lie!" My voice shook, and my hands trembled. I didn't notice the Ibis's approach until she was at my side. I never thought the presence of my rival could be such a comfort. Then Besa padded over and nuzzled my hand. I drew strength from them. Funny what a day could do. One moment you're worried about a high score; the next you're reeling as you find out your family isn't who you thought they were.

But it wasn't Uncle Moti who answered.

"You are speaking to the greatest general Axum has ever seen," Kamali hissed. The bunamech helped her cross the room to stand by Uncle Moti's side. "He saved us. He saved you. Then he raised you, cared for you, taught you, *provided for you*. You would have died had you stayed. So what if he doesn't share your blood? Does that make what he did any less important? Isn't that what family would do? Your parents —"

"Kamali."

The one word cut off the pilot's tirade, her face growing tight as she realized she'd been about to divulge something. Something that rocked my already-fragile grip on the day. Something I was very curious about.

"What about my parents?" I asked, my voice barely above a whisper.

Uncle Moti shook his head. "Now is not the time."

"No, no, no. I think this is the *perfect* time to discuss this. You told me they couldn't raise me. That they didn't want me sharing their name. You told me to forget about them. To pretend they didn't exist!"

"Yared, we have work to do."

"But —"

"ENOUGH!" The shout filled the room. Uncle Moti took a deep breath. "Someone has to go to Axum and warn them. Bring back reinforcements. It's too soon; everything is moving too fast. I'd thought we would do this together, that I would reunite you with them if I just had enough time." He balled a fist and hammered it into his other palm, his head bowed. Then, suddenly, he whirled, dropping to one knee with a wince and placing both hands on my shoulders.

"Yared, I'm so sorry. I failed you. I have to make this journey alone. One day — soon! — you will see your parents. I promise."

See . . . my parents? I stumbled backward, the world shifting beneath my feet.

"General?" Kamali was saying.

Uncle Moti shook his head. "We'll rest now. In the morning, Yared will command Besa to lead me to the last hidden gate of the Emperor of Axum. Tonight they should remain as they were. Just in case . . ." His voice trailed off, and he cleared his throat. "But if we don't get help, the Werari dogs and their monster will crush us once and for all."

"General, no." Kamali turned to him, wincing as she held her ribs. "Your leg. You will never make the climb. And if you do, and they discover you, they will . . ." Her voice trailed off at Uncle Moti's expression. A hand reached up, as if on its own, to touch his face. Then Kamali seemed to remember the Ibis and I were watching, and she let it drop. Some unspoken communication passed between them, but I was too shook to process it.

My parents.

Axum.

I bit back the rest of the hot anger that threatened to spill out of me. So many lies. So many half-truths.

My parents. Axum.

A day ago, I'd thought both were feel-good bedtime stories. Now . . .

I looked up. My eyes strained to look

past the metal ceiling. Past the Gebeya. Past the Authority's drones and the clouds above them. There. The stars. Space. Axum. My parents. My eyes dropped to Besa, and I thought of the map she had.

"Yared?"

I looked up to see everyone staring at me. Uncle Moti tossed me a sealed packet and pointed to one of the portable cooktops. "Heat up some sambusas for you and your friend, then grab a bunk. We'll have to figure out what to do with you tomorrow."

"Um, General?" The Ibis raised her hand. "What about my farm? My mother and father and sisters might be in trouble and —"

But Uncle Moti's head shake cut her off. "I'm sorry. We can't spare the resources to send anyone to your home, and it's too risky to let you return. It might bring even more unwanted attention to them." He glanced at me, then looked away. "Sometimes, you protect the ones you love by staying away."

The Ibis's face fell, and Uncle Moti's voice softened. "We will get you back to your farm after this is all over."

"You mean after I give away my oldest friend, and the two of you go find my long-lost parents in the fantastic sky city I recently discovered existed?" I spat out the question. Uncle Moti's face grew angry, then fell into exhaustion and regret. He turned back to the screens. Kamali looked back and forth between the two of us, but I was already headed to the cooktops.

"Come on," I muttered to the Ibis.

Kamali and Uncle Moti (the great and brilliant general, long may he rule over spoiled twelve-year-olds) began to talk in quiet whispers. I squatted over the cooktop, powered it on, and dropped the foil packet onto the surface. I flipped it every so often, until steam began to wisp out of the corners and the smells of spicy vegetables and flaky crusts filled the air.

"Yared?" the Ibis asked.

"Hmm."

"I can't stay here. Who's going to protect my sisters if the Werari come for them again?"

"Oh, don't worry," I said, sliding open

the pouch and passing her a hot sambusa. The triangular pastry melted in my mouth as I took a bite. I swallowed, savoring the delicious treat, then opened a second pouch and reached into my pocket, pulling out the bundles of Sleep-Tree leaves I'd taken from the Ibis's family farm. I grinned sharply and nodded at Besa, who yowled uncertainly. "We're going to get help for your sisters — for all of Addis Prime. As soon as they nod off, we're going to Axum."

CHAPTER EIGHT

"This was a horrible idea."

The only thing more difficult than sneaking out of a secret bunker hidden deep within a floating maze of tunnels and berbere spice was doing it with a clumsy metal lioness. Seriously. Like, I could've scooted around with pots and pans glued to my bottom and made less noise.

The Ibis stood at the end of the tunnel, one hand resting on her skysail, the other motioning us to hurry up. "Would you two come on?!"

I braced my back against Besa's left flank, careful to avoid one of the spines inches away from my ear, and set my feet against the tunnel wall. "Okay, you giant mousetrap, we're doing this one more time. On the count of three, you pull and

I push. Got it?"

"Mrowr."

"No, *I* push; *you* pull. Focus! Here we go. One. Two. THREE."

I heaved, shoving myself backward, as the sound of metal scraping on metal echoed up and down the dark tunnel. I winced. If that noise didn't alert someone, nothing would. We had to leave, and quickly. Finally, with one last yowl, Besa's left rear paw popped free of the narrow gap in the floor she'd stepped into. She licked it, then carefully moved the few remaining paces to where the skysail waited.

The Ibis looked at me, then at Besa, then back at me. "Um, you *do* know she's not gonna fit, right?"

"Hey!" I covered Besa's ears. "Don't be rude."

"Yared."

"Okay, okay." She did have a point. Besa's new armor covered her chest plate and flanks, and even her tail now sported a weird curved spike at the end. The lion cub emblem we'd seen floating on the map was now emblazoned in the center

191

of her chest plate. All in all, my lioness looked as if she'd grown 50 percent larger in the course of a day.

I scratched my head. "Maybe we can tow her?"

The Ibis rolled her eyes. "Please be serious."

"I am! Look, we need her. She has the map, and I'm not leaving her behind with *them.* Maybe if she, like, I don't know . . . edges along the roof?"

CRASH.

Besa had taken a step forward, and this time her front paw pierced a loose piece of flooring. Her new claws sliced through the corrugated metal like a knife through niter kibbeh. The Ibis and I stared at the wickedly sharp claws, then at each other. I swallowed nervously. "Okay, maybe not the roof."

A skittering noise echoed down the tunnel behind us. We froze.

Well, the Ibis and I did. Besa dropped into a crouch and disappeared. One second she was stuck in the floor; the next I couldn't even see her. I could hear her, though. There was a low growl, then the sound of paws racing away, back down the tunnel. There was a loud squawk, then silence.

"Besa?" I whispered.

Nothing.

Just when my heart began to thud in my chest, my lioness flickered into view several meters away. She came padding up to me with her head held high, tail flicking self-importantly behind her, with a —

"Is that a giant bird?" the Ibis asked.

I sighed. One of those long, deep, incredibly exhausted sighs you let out when someone you love dearly does something so ridiculous that you want to yell at them, but it's so on brand it's not even worth it. Like, in all honesty, I really should have expected this.

"It's an undertaker bird. Besa . . . well, she has this thing with them. It's like a vendetta, except not as cool. Hey, drop it! Drop the giant bird, Besa!"

Besa growled and I shook my finger at her.

"Don't sass me. Drop the bird."

She spat out the undertaker bird, which

was just another name for this giant stork that loved to hang around the Gebeya and pick through the leftovers. It must have been picking through the debris, searching for food in all of the mess. The butcher shop outside probably seemed like a buffet. Somehow it entered the tunnels . . .

Wait.

That meant there was another way out of here.

The bird had a beak that looked like a spearhead, and it clacked it at us several times before stalking away back into the darkness.

I turned to the Ibis and forced a wide smile onto my face. "Well, on the bright side, now we know Besa can go into stealth mode and no one will ever know."

The Ibis approached Besa carefully. "Let me see that keyboard again."

But Besa just stared at her.

"Oh, right," I said. "Besa, she's fine. I, um, give you permission to let her help us. Authorized by Yared TheGr8. With a number not letters. Execute."

Now both the Ibis and Besa were star-

194

ing at me.

I sighed. "Look, I'm new at this; give me a break."

Besa rumbled something in her throat (pretty sure it wasn't polite), and the virtual keyboard connected to the lioness's programming appeared in the air. The Ibis keyed in a few commands before nodding. "Okay, long-range comms are active. As long as she stays within five hundred meters of the skysail, she can link with the ship's navigation system. This way we can follow her."

I clapped my hands together. "Excellent. I have a good feeling about this. Nothing could possibly go wrong, I'm sure of it. Everyone ready? Good. Follow that bird!"

The undertaker bird's secret exit turned out to be a ventilation shaft that led straight up to the top of the Gebeya. At first it wasn't wide enough for the skysail to enter, but you'd be surprised what a determined Guardian could do. I guess that's what I had to start calling Besa. But as she clawed upward, aiming for the bright white circle hundreds of meters above us, I kept trying to ignore a thought that fluttered around inside my mind.

Why exactly did I need guarding?

"You're doing it again." The Ibis nudged me, pointing to my side of the skysail. I cleared my throat, peeked out, then gave her the thumbs-up that we were all clear to keep rising upward. Besa had widened the shaft above us, and the lioness climbed out ahead of us, fading into stealth mode as she prepared to descend to the streets below and act as a guide to the gate to Axum.

"Doing what?" I asked.

"You've got that look on your face, the one you get when you're nervous but determined. *And* you're drooling."

"I do not drool," I said, wiping the corner of my mouth.

"You do when you're worried about something. It's your tell."

"See, that's how I know you're lying, because I don't have a tell."

The Ibis smirked. "Anytime you're about to do something foolish in HKO, your eyebrows scrunch and your eyes squint, and a liiiiiiittle bit of drool runs down your chin. Like you're so lost in planning your next move, it's almost as if you zone out. Pretty cute. Except, you know, for the whole drool part."

I wiped my mouth one more time, just to be sure, even though I was 99 percent positive she was making it up. (Okay, maybe 98.5 percent positive.) Still, it didn't hurt to double-check. *Wait, did she say cute? Uhhhhh.* But before I could respond to *that* little nugget of information, she pointed upward.

"Look, we're here."

The skysail rose out of the now-Besa-approved ventilation shaft slowly. Pink clouds greeted us from above, as Addis Prime began to welcome a new day. The Ibis rotated us slowly about so we could get our bearings. The tallest peaks of the highlands ran from the west to the north, their tops lost in great fog banks. Beneath us, the different woredas stretched out and began to get ready for the day. Hovercans headed toward the Gebeya, buna-mechs marched to their posts to greet pedestrians, and tuk-tuks lined up on the different streets, their thrusters keeping them bobbing in the air as they waited for their first fares of the day. South of us, the last of the great orbital farms were lifting off, heading out on the predetermined flight patterns that would get them the best sun and altitude for their coffee and teff crops. As they lumbered into the air, several Authority drones circled them, scanning for stowaways. I glared at them. Vultures.

"All right," the Ibis said. Her hands flew over the controls, and the map to Axum flickered into view. "We've got the signal from Besa."

I leaned over to peer beneath us. I couldn't see anything except for faint traces of black smoke from still-smoldering sections of the Gebeya. "Where is she?"

"Right . . . about . . . here."

A golden shield with a roaring lion appeared on the map. The Ibis enlarged it so we could zoom in on Besa's location. She was currently racing down a back alley in the residential district north of the Gebeya. The Ibis whistled. "Was she always that fast?"

I shook my head, words failing me. She was moving faster than an exo!

The Ibis muttered under her breath, then grabbed a mic from above her head. "Hey, metal butt! Slow down; we can't move as fast as you!"

But Besa continued to sprint. The Ibis sent us swooping down around the curve of the Gebeya. "You've got to control the camouflage," she said, both hands gripping the controls. "We can't go too high because the beetles up there will lock onto us. But keeping the camo on while going this fast will drain all our power. If we get out in the open, flip that toggle." She pointed at a red switch in front of me. "Then switch it off when we get back into cover. Just know that if it's on, we can't go as fast, so be careful!"

"Got it," I said, nodding. We zoomed down to a crowded corner, where a bunamech was handing out cups of coffee to passersby. I flipped the toggle. Nothing happened. I could still see the roof and the floor and the controls. I flipped it again. "Hey, I think it's broken."

"You can't see it from inside!" the Ibis shouted at me.

Shouts of surprise rang through the streets as we blew over the crowd. A few kids ran after us, laughing and extending their arms like wings. I winced. So much for being stealthy. "Sorry," I said as the skysail rushed into a neighborhood service alley used by delivery drones.

We followed Besa north, zipping in and out of alleys and keeping to the shadows. I got the hang of being a copilot and shouted out shortcuts while keeping an eye on the map. Besa didn't get too much farther ahead, but we weren't exactly gaining on her, either. The chase continued as the neighborhoods grew more and more sparse and the northern foothills grew closer. Finally, we left Addis Prime behind completely. The rocky slopes of the highlands flew beneath us, tall reddish-brown outcroppings nearly scraping the bottom of the skysail. I checked the map. Besa had slowed and started zigzagging, as if she were searching for something in particular. She stopped, and I grinned.

"I think we're almost —"

Alerts shrieked inside the skysail.

Four red dots appeared on the map, close on our tail. The Ibis looked over, but she had to focus on piloting around the towering trees and rocky hills of the highlands. "What is it? The Werari?"

I shook my head, then turned around to look. "No. Beetle drones."

"Would you stop staring out the window and help me?" the Ibis shouted. She sent the skysail zipping around the hills and in and out of the sparse trees dotting the slopes. The sun had finally risen, and the new day didn't seem to be starting any better than the last. A tad worse, actually.

I couldn't help but stare at our pursuers. The beetles flew in a diamond pattern. They kept a uniform distance from each other, maintaining perfect discipline as they hunted us down. The Ibis couldn't shake them. And she tried — we flew between trees, around boulders, and through deep ravines.

"What do you want me to do?" I shouted back at her. "Send them a firm note of disapproval?"

"Do *something*. We're running out of power. Once the reserves are tapped out, we're done for." As if on cue, the skysail shuddered, then hummed back to life.

We were running out of time. I bit my lip. Besa was still searching down below, moving in circles at the base of what looked to be a steep mountain. A *really* steep mountain. I frowned. Actually, it was more like a cliff. And were those — yes, giant, rough-hewn stairs were carved into the side! They led up diagonally in one direction, before reversing and climbing in the opposite, zigzagging all the way up the nearly vertical surface to a dark splotch near the top.

I gasped.

It wasn't a splotch. It was a doorway. And that wasn't a cliff . . . it was a tower. Old and worn down by the elements, but definitely a tower. And if I wasn't mistaken, it wasn't the only one.

"I know where we are," I said.

"What? Where are we?"

"The Ghebbi Fortress. Except . . ." I bit my lip. "I don't think it's a fortress at all. Uncle . . . *General* Moti used to say you could march to the stars if you hiked up to Ghebbi. What if . . . what if that wasn't just a saying?"

The Ibis glanced over at me. "You think

it's something more? Something to do with Axum?"

I nodded. "What if Ghebbi is actually an old spaceport?"

The Ibis opened her mouth to argue, then stopped and thought. "You *would* need a spaceport to launch and dock supply ships and personnel, especially if Addis Prime was once part of Axum."

"Exactly," I said, pounding one fist into my other palm. "That has to be where the last gate is." More proximity alerts blared in the skysail, and I gritted my teeth. "But we have to lose these beetles first, or we'll never get to Axum."

The Ibis tried to double back, but the beetle drones spread into a shallow claw shape, keeping us in front of them as they began to surround the skysail. Something in their formation looked familiar.

"A pincer trap," I whispered.

"What?"

I pointed at the drones. "It's a pincer trap. Uncle Moti — I mean General Moti — had me study this when I was in between schools. We moved a lot."

The Ibis shot me a quick look of disbelief before returning to the controls. "You studied battle strategy and maneuvers?"

"Sounds funny, and I complained at the time, but now I wonder . . ." I shook my head. Thoughts on what the man who raised me intended could come later. Right now I had to focus. "Whatever. The point is, the pincer trap is a risk for both the attackers and the defender. If the defender — that's us, by the way — gets completely surrounded, we're toast. But if we can spring the trap . . ." I grabbed the mic and shouted into it. "BESA! We've got drones on our tail. Execute the shambush plan!"

The Ibis stared at me. "Shambush?"

"Yeah. Like, it's an ambush and a sham at the same time. Shambush." I stopped when I saw the utter confusion on her face. "Just trust me. Fly to Besa. Full speed. When I say so, dive toward the ground."

Something started beeping on the controls. The Ibis gulped. "I hope you know what you're doing, because this is it. We're out of power."

The Authority drones zoomed closer and closer. Soon they would be in laser range, able to knock us out of the sky like swatting a gnat. I licked my lips. We had one shot. If we messed up, or if I mistimed it, or if Besa lost her balance like the last time we tried this, well . . . I glanced down. It wasn't too far of a plunge. Just a couple dozen meters.

"Yared," the Ibis said. She sounded nervous, too.

"Almost."

"They're warming up the lasers."

"Almooooooost."

The skysail shuddered again, and like that, the beetles were in range. "Now!" I shouted, and several things happened at once.

Each drone fired their laser.

The Ibis shoved the controls forward, sending us hurtling downward.

And an earsplitting roar cut through the air.

A silver blur hurtled past us. I whirled around in awe as Besa landed on the top of the falling skysail, gathered herself, and then leapt toward the drones. The lasers missed. Besa didn't. Four swipes, four hits. Bits of glass and black metal sprinkled the hills as the smoking drones fell to the ground. Besa landed on all four paws, unharmed and looking smug.

I wish I could say the same about us.

The skysail crashed through a stand of trees, skidded down a slope, and came to a jarring stop thanks to a boulder. The Ibis groaned. "Remind me to never, ever volunteer to be your partner again. Ever."

"What? That was fun." I levered myself up, then popped open the skysail canopy and hopped out. "Besides, we're here."

The Ibis followed. "How can you be so sure?"

I pointed to the humongous lake at the bottom of the mountains. "The sky's mirror." Then I pointed at the dark entryway at the very top of the cliff. "The last gate." Besa trotted over, black flecks of paint on her jaw. Someone had fun on their hunt. I patted her flanks and rubbed behind her ears. Then I stood and took a deep breath.

"Okay," I said. "Time to go ring Axum's doorbell."

CHAPTER NINE

The massive sandy-brown tower of the Ghebbi Fortress loomed overhead as the Ibis and I caught up with Besa. My lioness was sitting on her haunches, one paw scraping at a dusty brick. Each block was nearly as large as she was, and there were thousands of them interlocked together to form the rough cylinder structure. The sun beamed down on us overhead, and my stomach grumbled. We hadn't eaten since the sambusas last night.

"All right," I said, patting my stomach with one hand and wiping beads of sweat from my forehead with the other. "How do we get up those stairs?"

There was in fact a carved switchback leading to the dark entrance high above, but at several points, it stopped near what appeared to be tunnels into the fortress.

The beginning of the stairs started at one such tunnel entrance, nearly a dozen meters off the ground. Were we supposed to climb the tower wall to get there? Jump? Wish ourselves up?

"What is it, Besa?" I turned to find the Ibis crouched next to Besa, who was still pawing at a section of the tower brick and huffing softly. Besa looked at her and yowled. I wrinkled my brow and stepped over to where they were.

"She says the wall won't be quiet," I said.

The Ibis frowned. "What does that mean?"

"I don't know."

Besa swung her head to me and nudged my shoulder. "Mrrowr."

"Oh, it won't stop asking the same question. Sorry."

The three of us stared at the brick wall for several seconds. Somewhere in the foothills, the lilting call of a secretary bird carried up to us. A faint breeze tried to offer a cool respite from the climbing heat, but it gave up after a few limp gusts. Far up the mountain range —

"Wait, why is the brick talking?" I asked. "Bricks shouldn't be talking. They're like toes."

"What?" the Ibis asked, confused.

"Never mind. The point is, why does Besa think this brick is talking?"

Besa stood on her hind legs and pawed at the rough surface with both front paws. I shook my head and sighed. She was determined to dig through the wall! If I didn't do something, she was going to blunt her claws, and I for one did not want to be the person who sharpened them.

"Okay, Besa," I said, stepping forward and patting her. "That's enough."

"Wait." The Ibis had stepped forward, too, and she placed her ear next to the furrows Besa had clawed into the tower brick. "I think . . ."

"Not you, too," I said with a groan.

"No, feel." She grabbed my hand and pressed it flat against the wall a couple of meters away.

I shook my head. "I don't feel anything."

"Exactly. But if you come over here . . ."

She dragged my hand next to the claw marks, and the hairs on my arms stood straight up. I could feel it. A faint, pulsing vibration that stopped after a few seconds, then repeated. It was as if . . .

"Yared, you complete fool," I said. I stepped quickly over to Besa and activated her virtual keyboard. "Of course the back door to a spaceport wouldn't be in plain sight. It would be hidden. Disguised. Especially if it was a back door that only Guardians like Besa could find. It would only reveal itself if we knew where to look and had the key."

"The key?" The Ibis peered over my shoulder. I stepped aside to show her.

"Besa said the brick is asking a question, but it's a bit more than that. The entrance is asking for authentication. Now where did I see — Ah, got it." I highlighted the section in Besa's Guardian Protocol that was labeled Clearance Codes and hit execute.

A rush of air hissed out of the cracks of the tower's bricks, sending a shower of dust into our faces. I stumbled backward, coughing and rubbing at my eyes. "Blecchh. Eww, I think I swallowed a pebble. Besa, next time take us to the VIP entrance, please."

But when I cleared my eyes, Besa and the Ibis were staring at a two-meter-high doorway outlined in pulsing silver light. The door itself was golden, and light seemed to bend and refract around it, giving it a molten quality. Before I could gather my words and form a sentence of incredulity, Besa crouched, leapt forward, and disappeared.

"Besa, wait!" I started after her, but the Ibis grabbed my arm.

"Yared, hold on. Are you sure it's safe?"

I shook my head. "No. Not in the slightest. But I can't leave Besa alone. If this is how she says we get to Axum, then this is the way I go. Are you coming?"

I held out my hand. She stared at it, then let out a frustrated sigh. "Your foolishness is starting to rub off on me." But she grabbed it and squeezed.

I grinned. "Same time. On the count of three."

She rolled her eyes. "Not this again."

"One. Two."

And we jumped through.

We landed in a different world.

A long square tunnel curved up and out of sight. Glowing seams of light embedded in the four corners illuminated the passage. There was so much to take in I couldn't breathe. The walls alternated between the sheer mountain rock and floor-to-ceiling panels the color of burnished steel. Bas-reliefs depicting different scenes had been carved into the stone, while the metal panels remained blank unless we stood directly in front of them. But once we did . . .

The Ibis let out a soft gasp of surprise when the panel to our left came to life. "It's a screen," she said.

I stepped closer. Sure enough, it was an older model, but still a vidscreen. As we watched, images swirled into view. A single ship soared over tiny buildings and into the sky. A clear sky. No Authority beetle drones. No exos chasing them. Just a ship. It soared straight up, through clouds and up into the stars. There it joined a convoy of other ships, some larger and some smaller, all on their way somewhere. The ships disappeared off the left edge of the panel, and then the scene went blank. After several seconds, it started to repeat.

"Mrowr?"

I looked up. Besa stood halfway around the next bend in the passage, her ears quirked in a question.

"Sorry," I called out. "Just looking at the decor."

The Ibis had moved to the next panel, five or six paces farther up. "Look," she said. "The ships. They're heading to this giant structure."

I moved to her side. She was right. The next panel showed a giant rotating tower, wider at the bottom and narrowing to a point at the top, with two sets of wheels and spokes separating it in thirds. As it rotated, the ships from the previous panel approached, but it wasn't until they started to dock that I realized just how big the space tower was. The ships that had dwarfed buildings were now barely seen behind the rings they docked with. Dozens and dozens of vessels landed. The Ibis stared in wonder.

"It's a space station. It has to be."

"Not just any space station," I said grimly. Something about its design poked at my memory, but I couldn't figure out why. I did know one thing. "That's Axum."

We continued on up the passage, stopping to watch more of the scenes while Besa kept an eye out for danger. It was like one of Mrs. Marjani's living history lessons, when she would set up the AR projector and walk us through important moments in Addis Prime. Except those were boring, sleep-inducing lectures about teff irrigation methodologies. This . . . this was breathtaking. Awe-inspiring.

The space station sending scout ships out in all directions.

A close-up of one of the ships, landing on a planet nearly covered in oceans.

The ship taking on passengers before lifting off.

The space station again.

Inside, a grand receiving room the size of Addis Prime. People were lined up for miles, all waiting to see three figures standing on a platform that hovered in the middle of the room. A man, a woman, and an infant in the woman's lap. They were welcoming the new arrivals, I realized. I studied the family.

"Yared," the Ibis called. She was nearly around the next bend. When I jogged over, she pointed. A giant door waited at the top of the tunnel. Besa stood next to it, waiting for us to approach. I hadn't realized we'd walked so far.

"Look." Her voice trembled.

"Are you okay?" I asked.

"Just . . . look."

The final panel was blank. Then, as I stepped closer, a flowing script appeared, tracing itself horizontally. It was a familiar dialect, but I couldn't place where I'd seen it before, not until I read the words aloud.

Welcome, travelers . . .

You have reached your final home.

I stopped reading there, not because the words had stopped appearing, but because I realized what had shaken the

Ibis so much. As the script continued to fill the top of the panel, the image of the space station appeared at the bottom. It appeared piece by piece — first the tower, then each of its three rings. But it was when only the tower was visible that everything tumbled into place. For several moments, I couldn't breathe.

"Kaleb's Obelisk," I said. "It's Axum."

The gleaming black-and-gold tower that every player fought to reach in the HKO . . . it was the exact same tower as the one that now floated on the panel in front of us. But why? The Ibis must've been thinking the same thing. "Why would the HKO's designers base the final objective on a legendary space station?"

I pursed my lips. "Think about it. It's not just that. They named the shrinking ring in the battle royale after the Werari. And that adage of U . . . of General Moti's. It was the same thing the instructions would repeat. It's all connected."

"Yared," the Ibis said, placing a hand on my shoulder. "What are you saying?"

"I'm saying . . ." I took a pause, then let it all out. "I'm saying that HKO isn't a game. Or at least that's not all it is. It's also a message." I pointed at the tunnel. "All those old screens? They confirm it. Once, Axum spread far and wide, throughout the galaxy. But something cut it off, splintering it into what we are now. A city with old tech that hasn't advanced in years, and with a ban on all flying. All traces of Axum wiped from memory, except for the few who escaped whatever happened, like General Moti. How could we know how to return? Unless there was a message, hidden in plain sight."

I took a step forward to the giant door, my mind racing. A small silver grid appeared a meter off the floor, with the outline of a hand glowing in the middle. I squared my shoulders and stepped up to it. This was it. This was how I got to Axum. How I found my parents. Were they among the people we observed on the panels? Had the Werari — because who else could it be? — cut our family in half? Were they waiting for me, wondering where I'd gone?

Now was the time to find out.

"Yared, do you know what you're doing?" the Ibis asked.

"Of course," I lied. "I'm Yared the Great." And I pressed my hand against the grid.

CHAPTER TEN

"Standard authentication failed. Descendant authentication required."

The Ibis inhaled sharply, while I froze and Besa dropped into a crouch. We waited. Nothing happened. Not right away. But as soon as I took a breath and began to step back, thin metal binders appeared on either side of my hand. *Snik.* They crisscrossed and tightened, holding me tight. My eyes widened and I tried to pull away, but they wouldn't budge.

"Uh," I said. "Uhhhhhh."

The Ibis ran up to me. "Yared?" But before she could do anything to help, the floor started shaking. Giant squares of carved rock dropped from the ceiling, sliding down the tunnel walls. They covered the old vid panels, as if sealing them away.

Wait . . . sealing them away? My eyes widened.

"The grid must require a certain handprint, and mine wasn't the right one. The tunnel is closing itself off."

"Well, come on!" The Ibis turned and began to run back down the tunnel. "Let's get out of here! We can try again later."

"I can't; I'm stuck!"

She skidded to a stop and whirled around. "You're stuck? Why are you stuck?"

"I don't know *why* I'm stuck!" I shouted. "I didn't decide, 'Hmm, maybe I should take a bath in yasa tibs, get chased by a giant robotic ax-turtle, discover my only family member is actually a complete stranger, and, oh yeah, get stuck!' " More rocks began to descend. The floor wouldn't stop shaking . . . or the walls . . . or the ceiling!

And that's when a giant barrier appeared, not a meter from where we stood. Soon we'd be trapped in a space smaller than the hovercan I'd traveled in yesterday morning. "Ask the door why I'm stuck."

As if on cue, a voice spoke, soft and calm. "Voice authentication?"

Wait. I knew that voice. I closed my eyes, willing my pulse to stop racing and my heart to stop pounding. I looked at Besa, who'd stepped to my side, also staring at the grid with her head cocked. "So it's not just me, right?"

"Mrowr."

The Ibis joined us, looking around nervously as the rock partition continued to seal us in. Booming echoes filled the air beyond it; I could just imagine the tunnel slowly closing.

"Voice authentication?"

I know you. The thought popped into my head. That voice was . . . familiar. "Authenticate," I said tentatively.

Besa's speaker popped out. "Voice authentication?"

My eyes closed. My Zenaye system I used to log in to HKO. It had the same voice as the one from the door's security grid. That was strange. General Moti, back when he was still pretending to care about me, had helped me program the authentication system. He'd picked the voice, saying he'd stumbled across it. More lies.

"Yared?" the Ibis said. "We're running out of time." The floor was rumbling, and a force began to press down on me, as if trying to crush me into the dirt. Was the gravity growing stronger? I could barely stand. My head was light. The partition was nearly down . . . Were we running out of air? I couldn't let that happen. I *wouldn't* let that happen.

I tried to stand up straight. "Authenticate."

"Voice authentication?" Both the door and Besa's speaker spoke at once, in perfect unison, matching voice inflections and everything. I took a deep breath.

"Yared."

Seconds passed. Then: "Authentication failed."

I slumped, the gathering pressure nearly driving me to my knees, until I realized that only Besa's speaker had spoken. The door was processing my words. Of course! Besa's system thought I was trying to log in to the HKO, which had different credentials. I guess this door just needed my name.

A bright silver-blue seam of light pulsed around the door, and then the voice spoke again, soft and welcoming. But I couldn't hear the words. I also couldn't stand. My head felt so light and the pressure was so great that I started to slip into unconsciousness. The last thing I remember was the metal binds releasing me so I could drop to the floor. My eyelids fluttered closed as the door's familiar voice spoke happily into the room.

"Voice pattern detected, extrapolated, and age-matched. Welcome home, Yared."

I dreamed. A single lamp lit a small corner in an otherwise-dark workshop. Suitcases surrounded the workbench, and one of them was full of components made from the finest Axumite steel. A man hovered over the bench, tinted protective frames guarding his eyes. He wore a plain gray T-shirt beneath an unbuttoned pair of coveralls. His massive hands clutched a tiny welding torch and a curved bit of metal. He was in the middle of building something, his body hunched over the bench.

Uncle Moti, as I knew him then.

He was mumbling to himself, but he stopped suddenly and turned his head, standing upright.

"Come in, Yared," he said. "I know you're there."

I stepped into the light. My feet moved on their own. I didn't say anything, but Uncle Moti continued to talk as if we were holding a conversation.

"We have to leave in the morning. Yes, I know we just got here, but . . . things aren't working out. Have to keep moving. I know you're sad, and I'm sorry. I wish we could stay. Moving around like this — well, it's no way to raise you. I'm gonna do better, I promise."

He turned back to the table, then gestured me closer. "But look, I have something for you." Again, my feet moved without me. I didn't have control of this dream.

Yes, a dream. I realized that now. Or, more accurately, a memory.

I watched Uncle Moti use the seam torch to fasten the metal he held into place; then he stood upright and smiled. "Look. She's yours. Truthfully, you should've been gifted her a while ago, but . . . well, what's done is done. You've got her now."

A small lioness stood silent and still on the workshop bench. One of my hands rose to gently touch her head. She gleamed in the dim light, like a statue made of silver. Uncle Moti pressed a medallion into my hand.

"You activate her by authenticating yourself . . . go ahead. Call her name and then introduce yourself. Her name is Besa."

I could hear a voice speak — a boy's voice, no older than four or five. "Hi, Besa, welcome to our family. My name is Yared."

Yared.

Yared.

Yared.

"Yared. Yared?"

Someone was calling me from far away. I groaned and squeezed my already-closed eyes even tighter. There was a weird ringing in my ear, and that was drowning out whoever was trying to get my attention. Stupid alarm clocks. I just wanted to keep sleeping forever. I was having the best dream . . . Besa was in it, and Uncle Moti, and —

"Yared, get up! I can't find Besa!"

My eyes fluttered open. It took a minute for my surroundings to come into focus. A vaulted ceiling covered in glowing seams. Floating balls of blue light. A beam coming from somewhere to my right. Two faces standing over me. No, only one. After a few moments of blinking, my vision sharpened. The Ibis stared down with a concerned look on her face.

"Unngggh," I groaned. "Who put me to sleep?"

The Ibis sighed and held out a hand. I grabbed it, and she helped me to my feet. I wobbled for a second, then recovered my balance. "Not who. What. It's my fault. I'm used to it, and if I'd known, I would've prepared you for it."

"Whoa, slow down." I rubbed my eyes. It felt like I had a lingering headache lurking right behind the bridge of my nose. "What are you talking about?"

"This is a spaceport. You want to take off as high as possible, right? That was a lift we were on. But if you haven't been this high before, going up that quickly can be a shock to the system. That's why the tunnel was sealing itself off, because it had to regulate the atmosphere."

I looked around. We were in some sort of staging room, nearly as big as the old factory floor where I lived with . . . Moti. There was a door at the far side, but I ignored it for now. I couldn't help it. Everywhere I looked, I saw something that robbed me of my breath.

There were compartments built into the walls from which steam hissed and lights blinked green, amber, and red. Shelves stuffed with all sorts of gear lined the walls, including lightspears and war-bows like the kind Kamali kept. But what kept grabbing my attention were the slim tripod towers on which strange clothing hung — jumpsuits so black they absorbed light, and sleek metallic silver helmets with reflective faceshields. Displayed as they were on the outskirts of the room, they looked like an audience of judges silently assessing my worthiness. I stood a little straighter.

On the opposite side of the space, a viewing window let in that wide beam of light. I walked unsteadily over, the Ibis by my side. When I looked out, my knees buckled.

"Is . . . is that a cloud?"

The Ibis snorted, but she held my arm, making sure I stayed upright. "Yeah. We're above the Authority line. If anyone catches us —"

I swallowed. "Mrs. Marjani's detention will seem like a party."

Giant white clouds carpeted the sky fifty meters below the window. I couldn't see the ground, just the rest of the towers of Ghebbi Fortress piercing through. The sky shimmered a blue that felt impossible, free from the distortion of the Authority Net. I could drink in the view for hours, but the Ibis kept fidgeting next to me.

"What's wrong?"

She glared. "I told you, boy! I can't find Besa. She disappeared while I was trying to drag your butt in here."

Alarms blared inside me. I stepped

back and scanned the room. Now I felt the panic the Ibis was desperately trying to keep in control. Besa was a friend, a family member. Maybe the only family member I had. I couldn't lose her.

"Besa!" I shouted. I cupped my hands around my mouth. "Besaaa!"

"Yared," the Ibis whispered. "We don't know who's here. What if the Werari got here first?"

"I don't care," I said, the words coming out in a sob. "I have to find her. BESA!"

A faint roar echoed off in the distance. It came from across the room, where the door with the blinking red light stood, ominous and foreboding. I took a step forward, then paused and looked at the Ibis.

"Are you coming?" I asked.

She raised an eyebrow. "You're asking me? Not jumping into the pot with both feet and expecting me to follow?"

I shook my head. "This is different. I have to find Besa."

"I like the silly cat, too, Yared. Besides, I'm here now. These were the greatest astrogators in the world. In the galaxy! If you think I'm not going to explore, you're a bigger fool than I thought. And that's kinda hard to beat." I rolled my eyes. The grin she flashed at the end robbed the words of their sting.

"Fine," I said, walking over to the gear on the wall. "You're right, we don't know what's behind that door. Like you said, the Werari could've beaten us here. Or there might be automated exos set to repel intruders. There could be anything! So you have to do something for me."

"What?"

I held up a warbow in one hand and a lightspear in the other. "Choose your weapon."

"I get choosing a weapon. But . . . why did we have to put on the suits?"

The Ibis whispered the question as we crept down a brightly lit corridor. I looked down. It felt as if we were clothed in black holes. I was actually surprised it fit. But the staging room had been well stocked with suits available even for smaller frames. I guess you never knew who would be joining an expedition.

Axum had been ready to accept any and everyone who wanted to join.

Until they'd been attacked.

I slid up the faceshield on my helmet to distract myself. "Because they're cool?" I tried to strike a pose, but my fingers must've accidentally hit the inner controls. There was a loud *WHOOSH* and —

Well, how do I say this . . .

Thick gray foam shot out of hidden vents in the seat of my pants. I tripped, fell, and landed in a rapidly hardening blob. "Ah," I said. "And that would be . . ."

"Protectant for crash landings," the Ibis said with a sigh.

"Of course. I was just testing it out."

A snort was her only reply, and after a second, she extended her hand and helped me up. Before I could think of another joke or excuse to cover my embarrassment, a second roar echoed down the corridor. I gripped the warbow. I was always better at ranged combat in HKO. The Ibis held the lightspear at an angle behind her back in one hand, and I had no doubt she knew how to use it. Such a show-off. Another roar sounded. This time it was closer.

"Besa!" I took off running, ignoring the Ibis's yells.

"Yared, wait!"

The corridor turned at a ninety-degree angle to the right, and ended at a set of double doors. They were that same charcoal-gray color, and again a red light blinked above them. I sprinted closer, warbow fitted with an arrow, and just before I reached them, I dropped into a slide on both knees, pulling the bowstring back as the doors hissed open.

"Mrowr!"

The tension in the bowstring went slack, and the tip of the arrow drooped.

"Yared!" I heard the Ibis skid to a stop a few paces behind me. "Oh . . . my."

"Yeah," I said.

A curved metal platform as wide as a valley disappeared into the distance. Smooth tan walls that slanted slightly inward climbed to a ceiling so high it might as well have been the sky. Bright sunshine flooded inside through circular cutouts big enough to float the Gebeya through, landing on enormous elevated docking pads that dazzled the eyes with their brilliant white color. I counted twelve, and that's just before the platform curved out of sight. The docking pads were connected to the loading platform by curved tracks and hung suspended over a deep trench lined with craggy cliff faces. I couldn't help but admire how an entire spaceport had been disguised as a fortress in the side of a mountain.

But that admiration quickly faded at the sight of the giant robotic creatures standing in front of each docking pad. Four arms. Hydraulic and magnetic clamps at the end of each. A glowing red sensor ring instead of eyes. Each was mounted to tracks leading to the docking pads, able to move along them like motorized sentries.

Most were stationary, but one of them had its rusty, grubby fingers (okay, they weren't really fingers, just oversized magnetized pincers if we're being accurate) on Besa. It was in the middle of hauling her to a docking pad.

"Hey!" I shouted.

I started to raise the warbow, but the Ibis moved beside me and threw off my aim. She pointed to a raised circular station surrounded by several floating screens. "Look!"

"Not now —"

"Yes, now!" She grabbed my shoulder as a particular screen flashed red. "It's just like all the doors we passed through, remember? The warning lights?"

"So?"

"So we have a workstation like that back on the farm. They help us coordinate the orbital farms' flight patterns. Whenever a farm is coming to dock, we let everyone know by setting off alarms, and *flashing lights.* Now think — why would all the doors leading to the docking pads be flashing red warning lights?"

Her insistent tone made me pause, just for a moment. And in that moment, I realized what she was trying to say.

"A ship," I said softly. "There's a ship coming. From Axum."

She nodded. "It has to be. We must've triggered something when we arrived."

Another yowl of frustration echoed in

the giant space. Besa was still wriggling in the grips of the giant loader, and something clicked in my brain. "Not us. Her. A Guardian from Axum returning to a hidden spaceport. There had to have been protocols put in place for when that happened. Someone from Axum is coming to check it out. This could be our chance."

I took a step forward.

"Unauthorized personnel in the launch bay. Unauthorized personnel in the launch bay." A loud monotone filled the air, and I froze. I stepped back into the doorway, but it was too late. The sensor rings on the other robotic loaders began to glow red. All the way down the platform, every single one of those ridiculous oversized cleaning bots came to life, and all of them pivoted toward the two geniuses holding stolen weapons. There was no way this wasn't going to get ugly. So I had to be smart. I had to be careful. I had to be calm, cool, and talk my way out of this.

"Hi!" I said, waving my hand.

Unfortunately, it was the hand that held the warbow.

The loaders stood as one, their hover-rails unfolding into six scorpion-like legs. Their footsteps shook the platform as they clambered into a bristling, thirty-meter high wall of angry robot.

"Okaaaay," I said, slamming down my faceshield. "Talking isn't going to work, I see."

"You're not going to do what I think you are, are you?" the Ibis asked. But she already knew the answer, because she slid her own faceshield down and powered on the lightspear.

The bowstring went taut as I nocked the arrow and pulled it back to my cheek. "Don't really have a choice."

I let the arrow fly.

CHAPTER ELEVEN

Time slowed as the arrow soared through the air. I watched it, pride filling me. It was a perfect shot. The silver bolt streaked up and up, like lightning tipped with a diranium arrowhead. When the man formerly referred to as Uncle Moti had taught me how to use a warbow (because what family doesn't bond over high-stress archery simulations after dinner?), he showed how a well-placed arrow could take out the most difficult of opponents. I watched the projectile fly toward the giant loader bot with a grin already spreading across my face.

Tink.

The arrow bounced harmlessly off the bot's chin. Do bots have chins? I'd have to think about it later. Either way, the arrow did absolutely nothing. It fell to the right, disappearing into the yawning abyss. The Ibis cleared her throat.

"Soooo . . ." she said as the offended loader scuttled closer on its six legs, followed by the rest of its gang. "What was the next step in your plan? Tickle it?"

"No," I said. I grabbed her by the arm and pulled her aside, just as a massive pincer slammed into the platform where we'd been standing. "Run!"

I started to go left, and the Ibis ducked right. A giant foot attached to a steel leg the size of a tree trunk smashed down just in front of me. I spun right, only to crash into the Ibis as she tried to avoid a sweeping magnetic clamp aimed at her face. We tumbled to the floor in a heap.

Besa roared. I caught a glimpse of her struggling in the restraints as the giant drone floated away with her. "No!" I shouted, but a loader bot stepped into my path as I rolled to my feet. Its feet lifted and stomped on the platform in rapid succession, the impacts shaking the ground and forcing me to my knees. "BESA!"

"We have to . . . shut them down!" the Ibis panted, scrambling to her feet. The lightspear twirled in a blur as she jabbed it at a clamp that came too close. "There should be controls somewhere on that workstation up there."

The drone carrying Besa disappeared into one of the many openings in the wall. A panel slid shut behind it. I squeezed the warbow so hard it cut into the palm of my hand. I'd failed her. She'd had my back on so many occasions, and the one time she needed *my* help I'd let her down. If I couldn't protect her, did I even deserve her?

"Yared!" The Ibis grabbed my shoulder and shoved me. I fell head over heels, the giant clamps that had been approaching missing me by inches. "Get it together. If we shut these bots down, we can go after her!"

I stared at her. Go after Besa?

"We have to get to the workstation!"

The workstation? It floated a dozen meters off the floor, its thrusters firing gently to keep it bobbing in place. But a bunch of ticked-off scorpion loaders looking to make injera out of us stood in our way. Their sensors pulsed red as they crowded forward. We were running out of time and space, as the hostile ring shrank around us.

A shrinking ring.

"The Temple of Yeha campaign," I said quietly.

The Ibis, who'd moved to stand back to back with me, turned her head. "What? How can you think of HKO at a time like this?" She stepped backward, forcing me to move forward as a scorpion loader dashed at us.

"Do you remember that campaign? We had to reach the top of a sheer cliff face to find Kaleb's Obelisk, but only after defeating all those giant locusts and climbing on top of them? This is the same thing."

The Ibis pulled me forward, spinning me through a set of rusted legs as she dove through another. "Climb up the violent skull crushers? What could go wrong? And how are you going to get them to stand still for us to do that? Ask politely?"

"Nope. But I have an idea."

"Will it work this time?"

A foot nearly crushed me, but the Ibis

yanked on my suit, pulling me back in the nick of time. I flashed her a thankful smile. "Of course! I think."

"Yared —" she began, but I was already sprinting away.

I mean, honestly, how different were monstrous scorpion loaders designed by a legendary civilization of space-faring explorers from waist-high janitor bots with whirling scrub brushes? Deep down I'm sure they shared the same fear of a kid fouling up their mobility. They probably had nightmares about it. Botmares. Well, it was time to bring their fears to life. If I could avoid them and gunk up their wheels, we stood a fighting chance of getting out of here un-smooshed.

"Whoops! Thought you had me there, didn't you?" I dodged a leg, pulling the warbow back at the same time and firing it straight into a joint that I wanted to call a knee. But again, I wasn't sure about bot physiology. The arrow hit its mark, and when I ran away, the giant robotic scorpion bot tried to follow, only to have the leg jam up on the arrow. It stumbled, knocking aside a fellow scorpion bot that was chasing the Ibis.

She made a surprised face, then smiled. "Bet you don't bring down as many as me!"

"You're on!" I shouted.

We raced along the platform, angling toward the floating workstation with every step. I fired arrow after arrow, while the Ibis leapt off bent legs and climbed questing clamps, stabbing her lightspear with laser-like precision. Now I knew how Besa felt when she was trying to catch the little striped mice that skittered around the old factory. The scorpion loaders were just too slow.

CRASH.

Down went one.

BAM.

Another fell.

BOOM.

CLANG.

SKREET.

Three fell in quick succession, the last landing on the other two and filling the air with a squealing noise as metal rubbed on metal. There was only one more left. I could have laughed at the way it backed up as I approached, like an elephant trembling in front of a mouse. But it was still dangerous, and I couldn't get a clear shot at any of its joints.

"Come on!" I challenged.

And it did.

The scorpion loader's six legs hammered the platform as it rumbled forward, trying to bull rush me. I backpedaled, keeping a frantic eye on the edge of the platform behind me and the oncoming bionic giant. I was running out of space! I stopped just before the dropoff into nothingness and began firing arrow after arrow, hoping one of them would get lucky. But they all bounced off the scorpion loader's frame as it lowered all four arms, clamps slamming together in anticipation of squishing me.

What a way to go.

Then, just as it was meters away, the sensor ring on its head went dark.

It slowed, each leg raising and lifting as if in slow motion, before coming to a complete stop. One foot was raised in the air just above my head, poised to flatten me into a Yared patty.

"You're welcome!"

I scooted out from under the foot and looked up. The Ibis stood on the floating workstation, waving her arm cheerily. I let out a shaky breath. "What took you so long?"

"Well, first of all, I had to translate all the commands using only their pictures, and second, next time I'll let your scrawny behind get smooshed!"

I thought about that, then bowed. "I am forever in your debt, O great warrior."

"And you better not forget it. Now, come on, we just have to —"

Alarms began to blare. The loud sirens forced me to drop the warbow and clap my hands over my ears. I stumbled toward the workstation, but the Ibis was frantically pointing above me. By the time I realized she wanted me to hide, it was too late. I spun around and my jaw dropped open.

A sleek warship descended into the spaceport.

■ ■ ■ ■

Black like the night. Five thrusters — two at the front, two at the rear, one on the underside in the middle. Four mounted laser cannons that swiveled to train on me. And, most important, the silver outline of an S glittered on the side, right next to a series of characters.

"Is that who I think it is?" The whisper came through the earpiece in my helmet. I peeked over at the workstation, but the Ibis was nowhere in sight. She must have hid. *Like you should have, genius.*

I nodded, then realized she couldn't see me. "According to their call sign, that's the IAN *Ezana.*"

"You can read that?"

"It's Ge'ez," I muttered. Another language I'd studied. A hatch opened on the warship and two huge exos stalked out. I gaped at the power armor the soldiers of Axum wore. It was the same color as the jumpsuits the Ibis and I had borrowed (yes, borrowed), but that's where the similarities ended. A pattern rippled across their torsos as they stalked across the ramp, like a mesh weave made of starlight. The largest shotels I'd ever seen were strapped to their hips. Each of the pilots placed a hand on their hilts as they stopped several meters from me. Their helmets swiveled, taking in the carnage on the platform. I couldn't see behind their black faceshields, but I knew an angry adult when I saw one.

"So, what had happened was —" I began to say.

Shink.

The shotels slid from their scabbards, the edges of the curved blades rippling with inky black fire. I realized I still held the warbow, and I dropped it in a hurry, along with the few remaining arrows still in the quiver. The last thing I wanted was to appear as a threat.

Apparently it didn't matter. The shotel rose in the air.

"Wait!"

The Ibis leapt from her hiding place. Out of the corner of my eye, I could see her slide down the back of one of the scorpion loaders, flip off, pirouette in midair, and land in a crouch, lightspear extended behind her. "Leave him alone!"

Still the exo pilots didn't speak. They glanced at each other, then the one to my left straightened and stalked by me. I turned to watch, but the point of a shotel rose in front of my face.

Silent, shotel-wielding warriors from Axum. Why did that ring a bell? And these weren't the impostors from the Werari. These were the real deal.

The Meshenitai were deadly soldiers who fought to the death on behalf of the Emperor. No foe could stand before them. But the deadliest were those who fought in the Emperor's personal guard, the silent guardians of the throne.

Uncle Moti's (why couldn't I stop calling him that?) words echoed in my head. The Emperor's own guard! They could help! They could stop the Werari, and maybe even help me find my parents. I just needed to —

"Hey, let go of me!"

The other exo pilot had ripped the lightspear away from the Ibis. Now one gauntleted hand held her by the arm, while the other raised the shotel high. A whisper of movement drew my attention back to my own predicament. The shotel rose . . .

"Wait!" I shouted, lifting my faceshield. "Meshenitai! We need your help!"

The shotel froze.

I took a step forward. A tiny step. I wasn't a fool.

"You *are* the Meshenitai, right?" I asked. "The sworn protectors of Axum, of the Emperor and the Empress? We need your help. Right now, an army is tearing our homes apart. Uncle Moti and his friend — I think she's his friend, but maybe more? No, I'm gonna say just friends. Anyway, they both call them the Werari. And they've got this giant robotic creature that looks like a turtle and an ax had a baby."

The shotel lowered. "The Bulgu." A metallic voice echoed through a hidden external speaker. I blinked. What happened to being a silent soldier? I swear, some myths are just that, myths. The Meshenitai turned to where their partner held the Ibis. "Perhaps we should . . ."

"No," the other Meshenitai said. This

voice was a bit higher but still metallic and modulated, as if the external speaker had a loose wire causing a static-filled connection.

"But if what the loud one says is true —"

The loud one?

"It is a trick. Dispatch him, and let us disable this base as instructed."

"Wait!" I shouted. "It's not a trick. The Werari are real! They destroyed the Gebeya — well, that thing did. The Bulgu? Crushed it like a grape."

The warrior in front of me returned their shotel to its scabbard. I let out a sigh of relief. The other Meshenitai hissed a challenge. "Are you losing it? Our orders —"

"Our orders were to investigate and dispatch the enemy where encountered," my captor said. "Not attack children."

"Time has made you weak."

The closest Meshenitai's faceshield slid up, and a pair of brown eyes stared at me beneath bushy graying eyebrows. Wrinkles pulled at the corners like crow's feet. Then the warrior winked. "No, time has us seeing enemies everywhere. But not here, my dear. Not here."

The other warrior let out a snarl and raised their shotel, ready to slice through the Ibis. I whirled and sprinted over, but there was no way I was going to reach them in time. I could only stare as the blade descended.

A deafening roar blasted through the spaceport.

Shards of metal and rock exploded outward as a silver blur erupted from one of the loading compartments, racing along the hovering conveyor belt and streaking through the air. An armored beast landed on the platform and within seconds skidded to a stop between the Ibis and the shotel-wielding Meshenitai.

Claws like butcher knives and taller than me.

Golden armor with the same mesh weave as the Axum warriors.

The golden image of a roaring lion cub on its thick, armored skull.

Two amber eyes turned to me.

"Mrowr?"

I sank to my knees. It was Besa.

CHAPTER TWELVE

My lioness looked like she could have destroyed the scorpion loaders with no effort. She was easily twice as big as before, just moments earlier. What had happened behind the spaceport walls?

"Besa?" I said quietly. "Is that . . . ? Are you okay?"

I started forward, only to freeze when the second Meshenitai's shotel dropped in front of my face.

"Don't. Move."

Besa growled and padded forward. As she moved, the spikes protruding from her back rippled like stalks of grass in the wind. She nudged the Ibis with her shoulder as she passed, then growled at the warrior threatening her. The rumble in her throat was deep, much deeper than I'd ever heard. Besa moved forward, forcing the Meshenitai to back up several steps. When she was satisfied, the bionic lioness nudged the Ibis again, pushing her toward me. The two walked silently over, and I threw my arms around the neck of my oldest friend. She nuzzled me, then butted me with her head. I laughed.

"Okay, okay. I'm fine. But what about you? You look . . . larger."

"Mrowr."

"No, I didn't say that, I said larger. Did you get new armor?"

"Rowr."

"No, no, it looks good. I love it." She butted me again, and I hugged her once more, squeezing tight. "Don't you leave me again. You hear me? Don't."

Someone cleared their throat behind me. I stood, wiping the corners of my eyes. The Meshenitai who'd winked at me had taken off her helmet. An older woman with close-cropped, graying hair and a single jeweled earring looked around the staging platform. She tucked the helmet under her arm and mopped her brow with the back of her other arm.

I studied her as Besa moved to stand in between the Meshenitai and us.

"Well," the woman said. "This is more than I was expecting. Wouldn't you say so, Fatima?"

The other Meshenitai, helmet still on and faceshield still down, turned to stare at the woman. "Mother! No names."

"Oh, I think we're beyond that now, dear." The older woman cocked her head and studied me. Her eyes narrowed. She took a step forward, but Besa's growl stopped her. "Fair enough, noble Guardian. I understand." She backed up, straightened, and placed a hand over heart. "Allow me to introduce myself. I am Leyu, captain of the Imperial Meshenitai, warrior of Axum, and mother of one daughter . . . who just happens to be glowering at me. That is Fatima — Oh, put your blade away, child."

Fatima slammed her shotel back into the scabbard and stood with her arms folded. Even through her armor I could feel the glare she leveled at the Ibis and me. Then, without another word, she spun on her heel and marched to the edge of the platform.

"Wait!" I shouted in warning, then stopped.

Miniature thrusters embedded in Fatima's armor fired. She leapt across a couple dozen meters, easily. I mean, like I would hop out of bed, she hopped to the landing pad and disappeared inside the warship.

"O . . . kay," I said. "Is she okay?"

"Ha!" the captain said. "You should see her when she's angry."

The Ibis stepped forward. "Captain Leyu, we need your help."

Leyu pursed her lips. "Why do I think I will not like where this is heading?"

"Because it will require something you're not obligated to give," I said quietly. "Trust. Belief. But we're telling the truth. The Werari are coming. They're destroying everything and dragging away anyone who gets in their way."

"And if it hadn't been for his uncle and his partner, a lot more people would be hurt," the Ibis interrupted.

"One, he's not my uncle, he's the man formerly known as my uncle. Second, do you even know if they're partners? They

254

could just be friends. We shouldn't assume anything."

The Ibis rolled her eyes. "I swear, when it comes to anything *not* HKO-related, you're a toddler in a world of grown-ups."

I stuck my tongue out at her.

"An-y-way," the Ibis continued, "if not for General Moti and Kamali, we —"

Leyu stiffened. "Did you say General Moti? As in General Moti Berihun? Of the Burning Legion?"

The Ibis and I exchanged glances. "Yeeeeeah?" I said slowly. "That's what we've been trying to tell you. So if you could just —"

The shotel hissed as Leyu drew it from her scabbard, so fast none of us had time to react. Even Besa was too slow. Before she could let out a roar, Leyu struck. Her hand, straight and stiff in the shape of a knife, lunged out and stabbed at a spot just beneath Besa's neck. The lioness shuddered, then grew still. The captain turned toward us. Her eyes glinted dangerously, and she slowly circled the Ibis and me until she was between us and the exit. She scanned the spaceport, looked back at the ship, then gritted her teeth and faced me. A twisted expression had settled on her face. Regret?

"— let us come with you," I finished, still in shock.

The point of the shotel jerked toward the warship. "In."

The Axumite warship was unlike any vehicle I'd ever stepped foot on. Partially because their technology far surpassed anything Addis Prime could produce. I remembered the old lightscreens in the classroom the previous morning. (Was it only a day ago I gave a presentation about the very ship we now sat inside? It felt like a million years.) I pictured the Menelik drives on the bottom of the Gebeya, the ones the Bulgu had destroyed. What could Addis Prime have been if the Werari hadn't interfered?

Virtual displays made of different colored lights winked instantly into existence as I stepped aboard, then disappeared when I didn't linger. ("Proximity displays," the Ibis whispered.) In the next compartment, rows of collapsible exo docking harnesses lined each side of the wall. ("So they can drop fully armored Meshenitai at a moment's notice," the Ibis gushed.) We entered the flight compartment, where Fatima sat in a reclined chair — the pilot's seat, it looked like — surrounded by several floating screens showing external views, ship readiness, and other information.

"That's the Sidamo command configuration," the Ibis began to say, and I turned to face her.

"Look. I know you like ships. So cool! But if you could dial back the enthusiasm juuuuuust a bit until we figure out if we're in trouble or not, that would be *delightful.*"

The Ibis rolled her eyes. Fatima overheard me, and her pilot's chair lifted and spun around to face us. She'd removed her helmet as she prepped the *Ezana* for departure. I could see the resemblance between her and her mother. They shared the same golden-brown skin, and bright eyes that didn't miss a thing. She looked to be several years older than the Ibis and me. Her hand went to the shotel next to her, but then Captain Leyu stepped up behind us. The Meshenitai captain pointed to two seats in the far corner.

"Sit," she said. "And be silent."

We did, but then Besa walked in, slow and nonresponsive. I couldn't contain myself. I had to speak up.

"What did you to do Besa? Will she be okay?"

Captain Leyu didn't answer. She guided my lioness to a harness I hadn't noticed on the opposite wall. It had room for four legs, not two, and Besa stood idly as she was secured. I watched in growing frustration. The final straw was when the captain fitted a molded diranium muzzle over Besa's snout.

"Captain!" I shouted. "What are you doing? Answer me!"

The captain turned around, a look of fury on her face. I swallowed but didn't let up. "Look, I just want to know if she'll be okay. That's it. I've never seen her like this before, and I've had her my whole life. Whatever we've done, she was just protecting me. That's it."

Some of the fire in Captain Leyu's eyes flickered and eased, but it was Fatima who spoke. "The Guardian will be fine. She's just in stasis right now." She made eye contact with me, and I flinched at the hatred in her gaze. "You can thank your *uncle* for that. Because of him, no Meshenitai will ever be taken by surprise again. The traitor."

Traitor.

"Fatima," Captain Leyu said sharply, and her daughter fell silent. The older woman's eyes flicked upward and around the ship, then went back to Fatima. Her daughter swiveled the pilot's chair around and reclined, the light-screens winking back into existence.

"Launch in five," she said.

The floor began to rumble as the *Ezana*'s thrusters powered up. Next to me, the Ibis clenched her fists. When I looked over, her face was tight and her heels were bouncing up and down rapidly. I sighed. This was my fault. I had to try and tell her everything would be okay. Somehow, we would get through this. We'd convince Axum to help us, to free Addis Prime from the threat of the Werari. Time to be a leader. I reached over and placed my hand on her arm.

She looked up, and I tried to put on my best reassuring smile.

The Ibis frowned. "Are you constipated?"

A snort echoed from across the room, where Captain Leyu studiously avoided eye contact. "No," I said, glaring at the captain before returning to the Ibis. "I was trying to let you know that everything is going to be okay."

"Oh. Are you worried?"

"Well, you were looking anxious, so I thought —"

"Anxious?" The Ibis grinned. "I can't wait! Can you imagine? We're flying. Flying! And in the most advanced ship I've ever seen, or even read about. This is Axum! Think of the advances in flight capabilities." She slumped back in her harness with a sigh of something I was pretty sure was dreamy satisfaction. After a moment, she sat up. "Now, granted, this is all highly illegal. If we get caught, we'll probably never see our families again. Or Addis Prime — or sunlight, probably. But we're *flying!*"

Now Captain Leyu did laugh as she

looked over. "You sound like my daughter. You have the soul of a Meshenitai."

Fatima shot a glance over at us and raised her eyebrow. "That's all she will ever have."

Her mother sighed. "I'm afraid she's right, however rude the delivery. This will be a short trip. You will be deposed by Imperial Security, after which your fate will be decided. You made a grave mistake when you stumbled onto this facility. It should have been decommissioned a long time ago."

"But why?" I leaned forward, pleading. "Don't you care? The Werari have returned. They're destroying lives. We *need* you. For years, all my uncle spoke of was . . ." My voice trailed off at the expression on the Meshenitai's face. It was like as soon as I mentioned General Moti, uncontainable rage flared within Captain Leyu.

"So," she said. "Your *uncle* told you stories, did he? Stories of Axum's glory, no doubt. Of our decorated history and the peace spread by the Wings of Black, when ships traveled from planet to planet. He told you all that, did he?"

I nodded, unsure of where the knife in her words would strike. I didn't have long to wait.

Captain Leyu leaned forward, her eyes as hard as stone, her words as sharp as the blade she carried. "Did he perchance tell you of the night he betrayed those very legends, that history, and the people of Axum? Or did he leave that part out? Tell me, young warrior, did he tell you about the night fathers wept, mothers cried, and the children of Axum beat their chests and dripped tears in the night sky?"

She sat back, shaking her head at the horrified expression on my face. Now it was the Ibis's turn to place her hand on my arm. But I didn't need consoling. See, it wasn't true. It couldn't be true. There's no way Uncle Moti would have caused so much anguish. I mean, yes, he did lie about who he was, but that didn't mean he'd lied about everything, right? Right?

"I know it's hard to believe, child." It was as if she'd read my thoughts. Captain Leyu looked away. Fatima briefly caught her eye, before returning to the controls.

Her mother took a deep breath. "Sometimes we adults don't . . . tell the complete truth about everything. We leave parts out. The sin of omission — we've all been guilty of it at some point or another. All of us."

"Mother."

Leyu fell silent at some hidden warning in Fatima's voice. Her daughter slid her hands across the screens, and the thrusters went to full power. "Liftoff in ten," she said. "Nine. Eight. Seven . . ."

Captain Leyu looked at me, her expression unreadable. "Let *me* tell you this, then. The flight will be short, but there should be just enough time. Allow me to give you the truth General Moti Berihun conveniently left out."

General Moti Berihun created the Guardian protocol, and — I must say — for good reason. When he was a new Meshenitai recruit, there was an assassination attempt aimed at one of the members of Axum's Imperial Family. We couldn't have known then that the assassination attempt was a prelude to the Werari invasion. It was thought to be a power play by an estranged family member. Recruit Berihun, as he was called at the time, just so happened to be on patrol when a missile containing a monster flew right into the sky city's Imperial Palace.

The Bulgu emerged.

I don't need to tell you the destruction that monster caused. If what you've said is true, you've seen it for yourself. Chaos. Panic. Fear. Death. It was only by the drastic actions of Recruit Berihun that the palace survived. He flew a dropship into the monster's chest and carried it into the stars. Lives were forever changed that day. Everyone dealt with the losses they experienced in different ways. Family, friends, identity. For Recruit Berihun, it was his innocence. His belief in Axum's invulnerability was assaulted, and he never recovered. He decided that from then on, he would protect Axum — no matter the cost. That single-minded determination carried him toward greatness . . . or so we thought.

Moti Berihun rose through the ranks, redefining Axum military strategy as he did. Warship attack patterns, infantry formations, Meshenitai deployments — he increased our readiness with each passing day. He saw the Bulgu for what it was: not a one-time occurrence, but an opening salvo.

And he alone foresaw the arrival of the monster's owner — the Werari.

Axum wasn't ready. Humans make mistakes. Humans were supposed to be watching the displays when the Bulgu crashed onto the palace grounds. No, humans were too fallible. If Axum was to be protected, something more was needed. And what better way to combat a bionic threat than with a bionic protector?

Thus the Guardians were born.

They were lions built from the same material as our warships, with the ability to analyze threats and react faster than any human could. Together with a select group of Meshenitai, the now-general Berihun created the Burning Legion, warriors and Guardians working together with the sole purpose of protecting Axum. Not just the space station or our wealth or technology — but its people. Especially the Imperial Family, the only ones who could unlock Axum's most precious treasure.

But the general made one mistake — he thought he had more time.

I don't know why the traitor fled the palace on the night the Werari returned. Was it because the Guardian Protocol, his pet project, had failed when Axum needed it most? Possibly. But he took the key to Axum's naval power with him. Some have even said General Berihun aided the invaders, realizing it was futile to resist. I find that conspiracy theory hard to believe. However, there is a suspicion that I've long harbored, one that needs to be confirmed. Which is why we're heading to the beginning. Back to the spot where General Moti Berihun concocted the wild idea that would become the Guardian Protocol.

At Imperial Security, we shall find the truth.

Captain Leyu sat back in her harness, finishing her story. She stared at me with this weird look that was somewhere between anger and admiration. Like she wanted to yell at me for not living up to my potential — that thing teachers say when students who should be acing a class goof off and their grades suffer. Mrs. Marjani had certainly yelled at me about that on several occasions. Now Leyu the Meshenitai captain looked as if

266

she wanted to do the same. The thing of it was, she wasn't the only one looking at me like that.

Fatima stared at me from her pilot's seat high above the flight deck.

"What?" I asked.

Even the Ibis looked at me strangely from her seat next to me.

"What is it?" I checked to see if something had happened with Besa, but she was still unresponsive.

"Yared," the Ibis began, dragging me from my thoughts. Then she paused. "No, never mind."

"Oh, no you don't. You can't stop there. You were going to say something. What was it?" When she didn't answer, I threw back my head and let out a frustrated laugh. "You all want to say something, don't you? Well . . . let's have it! I'm not going anywhere. Apparently I'm destined for a small room with a tiny hoverlamp and scary grown-ups asking questions I don't understand."

Silence stretched throughout the flight deck. Fatima returned to her displays. "We're here," she called over her shoulder. She made a gesture as if she was flinging droplets of water from her fingertips, and one screen grew larger than the others. The Ibis watched it, awestruck.

"Adaptive intuition displays," she said as a glittering blue image moved to the center of the room. But it was what the screen *showed* that captivated me.

It was the obelisk from before, except . . .

"What happened? Where are the other rings?" I whispered.

It was the same obelisk from the Ghebbi spaceport, the one we'd seen while walking up the mountain path. Or, at least the top of it. The column was shorter, though the familiar pyramid still capped it. And there was one of the docking rings, but the other two had vanished. I shook my head. Something didn't feel right. When I turned to Captain Leyu, that feeling crystallized into cold, hard fear. She'd unsnapped her harness and grabbed my seat, drawing so close I could see each muscle in her face twitch. She wore a look of utter revulsion. Her expression twisted into a snarl that rivaled the Bulgu and she whispered, inches from my face.

"Divided and carried away, like the spoils of a petty dispute. The Werari's retribution for the actions of your 'uncle.' This is the legacy of General Moti Berihun. Families divided. Homes destroyed. All because he abandoned us in our hour of need. You say the Werari have returned? I say they never left. They were merely biding their time, waiting for the final piece of the puzzle that has prevented their spread across the galaxy."

She lifted my medallion from my head with one hand, shielding it with her body. "You."

I gawked. "What?"

"Think, child. I told you General Berihun fled with the final key to the Axumite navy. And yet it was more than that. He fled to the surface of the world we orbited and hid it in plain sight. Always thought he was smarter than everyone else. But it was only a matter of time before someone got curious about extraordinary technology floating in the middle of a city."

The Ibis inhaled sharply. Captain Leyu smiled, but there was no humor in it. "What?" I asked.

"The Gebeya," the Ibis whispered. "Yared, the giant Menelik drives . . . those are the engines of Axum."

I stared at her in disbelief. The Gebeya? The giant floating market? I pictured the five Menelik drives blazing — well, now three since the Bulgu's attack. At just 1 percent of their power, they kept the massive structure in place above Addis Prime. The column of light that filled the rectangular atrium had always looked unfinished, as if something belonged there . . . something like . . .

"No," I said. "Uncle Moti wouldn't take those. He wouldn't —"

"What?" Captain Leyu sneered. "Lie? No. Omit the truth? Well . . ."

The sin of omission.

The captain released herself from her harness. "But he needed something else. A key. Something encoding the centuries of astrogation data that guided our people through the stars, growing our nation, our family. Something like . . ." The captain walked over to Besa, passing through the holo of the giant obelisk space station in the middle of the flight deck. She pressed the black-and-gold

270

medallion into the slot on the lioness's head.

The medallion? That was the key?

"Authorization: Captain Leyu Shahai of the *Ezana,* Axum Imperial Security." She looked at me, then continued. "Guardian Protocol: temporary suspension."

"Temporary suspension of Guardian Protocol impossible. Only a member of the Axum Royal Family may disable the Guardian Protocol." The voice came from Besa's hidden speaker. Captain Leyu nodded. She walked over to me, the medallion now in her pocket. The one Uncle Moti told me to never lose, to protect as if it was my life, my legacy. And suddenly I realized why. The medallion wasn't the key.

"No," I said, shrinking back in my seat.

Captain Leyu stood in front of me.

"No!" I shouted.

The only ones who could unlock the power of Axum were . . .

. . . the Imperial Family.

General Moti Berihun fled with the key

to Axum's power.

Captain Leyu knelt, placing a fist over her heart and bowing her head.

"Welcome home," she said, "my prince."

CHAPTER THIRTEEN

One night, bored and alone in Addis Prime, I'd wandered off deep within the Oromo Prime district. It didn't take me long to get lost. When Uncle Moti finally found me, he jumped out of a still-moving vehicle to retrieve me.

I remember three things about that night. First, he drove us home in the old broken-down tuk-tuk he used to taxi people around Addis Prime. Back then he'd only had the one job, not like today when he worked three. And Uncle Moti is the most careful driver ever! It's like he hated doing anything that would draw attention to his driving, so he was super cautious. I always thought it was because he was a supreme rules follower, but I guess he was just trying to lie low.

He'd been so angry. I mean *super*

angry. So angry he nearly crashed the old tuk-tuk four times. Like, if eyes could shoot flame (in the real world . . . HKO had experimented with a pupil-scorching phase a few seasons ago and it did NOT go well, let me tell you), I would have been toast. Burnt toast. Incinerated toast.

The second thing that struck me about that night was his tears.

You've got to understand, Uncle Moti was the strongest person I knew. He could lift cars, fix anything. Every morning, he woke up before the sun to jog through the old factories and the abandoned warehouses where we lived. I mean, that's strong. Who got up first thing in the morning and ran . . . for fun? Not me.

So when I saw the tears streaming down his face, I realized just how much he'd worried. He didn't speak to me the whole ride, even when I tried to explain what happened. He just wiped away his tears and focused on steering the old two-seater hovercab back to our home. When we arrived, he cut off the tiny engine and sat back in his seat. For the first time in a while, I saw just how tired he was. How hard he worked. How much he did to keep a roof over our heads. It was at that point I made the decision to try and help out more. What good was making a name for myself if the person I cared about worked himself to death?

But the third thing, and maybe the most important, is that was the night he finally helped me upgrade Besa. We'd worked on her together, and I always knew he wanted me to have her, but that night he finally activated her Zenaye system.

"You need someone to keep you out of trouble," he'd said, crouching in front of me and placing my hand on the center of the lioness's forehead. "I know we move around a lot, and that it's been hard on you finding friends. Maybe if you have Besa . . . well, anyway. Here. Take this."

He handed me a black-and-gold medallion with a red jewel in the center, pressing it into my palm and folding my fingers over it. "Never let this out of your sight. It's the key to . . . Besa. Without it, we're all in big trouble. Got it?"

I'd nodded, overwhelmed. Who gets in trouble and then receives a gift? Let me tell you, I was stunned. Maybe even flabbergasted.

And to think it was all a lie.

"Now docking."

Fatima's voice filtered through the noise bouncing around inside my skull — the internal screaming, the replays of every conversation I'd ever had with General Moti, and the words of Captain Leyu.

My prince.

It wasn't possible. It was a lie. A dream. This totally sounded like something out of the vids Haji would sneak into Mrs. Marjani's class, one of those dramas where the suspiciously in-shape main character would take off his delivery hat and realize he was a hero. One of those *Chosen One* tales. Every kid dreamed of that. Oh, you're secretly the son of a spy. Oh, you're secretly the daughter of a flying superhero. Oh, you're the kidnapped prince of a space-faring empire's royal family, and you've accidentally triggered the resurgence of the deadliest war the galaxy has ever seen.

Oh boy!

My prince.

"Yared, are you okay?"

I looked up. The Ibis stood in front of me. The ship had docked, and Fatima was nowhere to be seen. As she leaned over and helped me extricate myself from the seat's harness, the Ibis whispered in my ear, "We could make a run for it. Maybe I can figure out a way to pilot the ship and —"

I shook my head. "No."

"You've got a plan?"

Again, I shook my head. "No plan."

She stared at me, confused. "So . . . what? You're just going to give up? What about Besa? They took her!"

Sure enough, the space where my lioness had stood was now empty. And yet . . . I felt nothing. No, that wasn't quite right. It's just that the ache I felt at her loss was swallowed by the void where my heart should have been. As the man who'd lied to me my whole life would often say, the gazelle doesn't notice its twisted ankle when it's being eaten by the lion.

"Yared?"

Oh, I'd faded back into my own head again. The Ibis stared at me, worried. I tried to put a smile on my face, but my lips quivered. I stood up and brushed past her. My hands dropped to my knees as I hunched over, trying to breathe. Everything was just . . . so much.

"Come, children," said Captain Leyu. I heard her footsteps approach and stood. She'd put her helmet back on, though the faceshield was up. She gestured at the door, indicating we were supposed to precede her. "My prince."

My prince.

Fatima waited for us at the bottom of the gangplank and took up her position to the side and slightly behind the Ibis. Captain Leyu mirrored her next to me. She pointed at a familiar floating pyramid, gently spinning a meter off the ground in front of us.

"Follow the guide," she said.

The pyramid began to spin faster. "Selam, Your Highness. Please allow me to escort you to the throne room."

I stopped. "Wait, throne room? I

thought we were going to be interrogated?"

The Meshenitai captain pursed her lips. "You are the prince. You've been summoned."

"Summoned? Why?"

"Well . . . it appears the Emperor and Empress wish to speak to you. I can imagine that after years of being separated from their only son, they *might* have some desire to see what has become of him."

She must have seen something approaching horror on my face, because she knelt down in front of me and placed an armored gauntlet on my shoulder. "You can do this, my prince. No one blames you for the traitor's actions. And besides . . ."

Captain Leyu stood and slid her faceshield down, her voice now coming from the exo's external speakers.

"You don't have a choice."

Axum.

A people of the stars, of ships and space and the blackness in between them all. A nation that accepted all, who built their civilization on the principles of community, of belonging, of family chosen and found. Everywhere I looked I saw the evidence for myself. The space station was so huge, it actually confused my mind. I couldn't accept just how large the structure was. We stepped onto a people mover that ran the length of the docking ring. Pristine white walls arched overhead, and there were hundreds of similar guideways anchored to loading platforms that must've once held thousands of people arriving off Axumite transports. I could imagine the noise. Babies crying. Kids playing and shouting. Adults nervous but excited. A home! But not us. We rode in silence, everyone in their own thoughts.

After some time had passed, we entered the section of the ring connected to what the spinning guide called the fifteenth residential section, or RS-15. When the Ibis asked how many the station held, the bot spun even faster.

"Currently, there are one hundred and five residential sections in operating condition, each capable of holding five thousand occupants — more if citizens cohabited in a single dwelling. This does not include the seventy-six residential sections currently in need of repair."

The Ibis whistled. "That's almost a million people!"

The people mover hummed along, exiting the matte-gray docking section and passing beneath a sign indicating the RS-15 Traversal Zone. We slowed down, and for a moment, I was confused, until I realized that the system still operated as though there were crowds in the zone for us to merge with. Families getting something to eat. Kids on their way home from school. Adults on their way home from work. They would all use the people movers to get around.

The void in my chest grew larger, swallowing even more pain as the impact of those numbers registered. People had lived here. Families. Friends. All gone because of the Werari.

We began to slow, and I looked around. The white walls of the residential section had been replaced by gold-trimmed silver panels, the image of a roaring lion engraved every so often. Guards patrolled, and I even saw a few Meshenitai clomping along the walkways, their exos polished to a perfect gleam.

"Now entering the Imperial Residence. Please wait for the vehicle to come to a complete stop before following." The bot paused for the people mover to grind to a halt, then floated down onto a wide walkway that stretched hundreds of meters in either direction. It led off into the center of the space station, where a sprawling estate waited.

"That's the Imperial Residence?" the Ibis whispered.

I shrugged. Seemed grand enough. Way bigger than anything back in Addis Prime. "Of course the rulers of a space empire would live in something that rich." I couldn't help but keep the bitterness out of my voice.

Captain Leyu overheard.

"Before you pass judgement," she said casually, "I would point out that the Imperial Residence also functions as a school, an assisted living home for those requiring aid, and a hospital. The Emperor and Empress have been very active in the care and well-being of Axum's citizens. Those who remain," she added at the end.

I started to walk up the path, leaving the others behind. "Let's just get this over with."

My prince.

My fists clenched. My parents. Royalty. I grunted. Haji would get a kick out of that. So would the other students in my class. Even Mrs. Marjani would think that was funny, and she'd do her snorting laugh that always made everything ten times funnier.

My steps slowed.

But nothing was humorous now. Soon they could all be more victims of the Werari. Who knew what the invaders and their Bulgu were up to at this very moment? If they'd decimated Axum to find me, what would they do to Addis Prime? And here I was, strolling for a meet and greet with my parents. Had it not been for the Meshenitai's shotel gleaming in the light of the station's simulated sun, it would've seemed like a dream.

Or maybe a nightmare.

I took a deep breath. Nearly there. I

had to get help for the people down in Addis Prime and the other woredas. The Werari must be stopped. Surely anyone could see that. I just had to convince my parents . . . and every kid knows that convincing adults to do the right thing was about as easy as performing a dental checkup on a crocodile. (This was an actual side quest during an earlier season of HKO. Don't ask.) But I was determined.

"Let's get this over with," I said. "It's just another parent-guardian conference."

The Imperial Residence bustled with activity as we approached the marbled stairs leading to a set of giant double doors. Gardening bots zoomed around, planting flowers or trimming shrubs, while several pairs of Meshenitai patrolled the grounds. Two stepped forward as I arrived, a scowl on my face, but they stopped when Captain Leyu waved a hand.

"He's expected," she said. "Transmitting clearance codes now."

The Ibis, who up to this point had been silently drinking everything in, now looked confused. "Clearance codes?" she asked.

The Meshenitai escorted us past the guards. "No one just pops up unexpectedly in the Imperial Residence. Everyone must have clearance codes at the time of their visit, even in the hospital or school."

"No ditching class to go play a game, I guess," I muttered.

At that moment, the giant doors swung inward, revealing a long, wide receiving hall. Light spilled inside, our shadows preceding us as we entered. It was dark. And huge. My footsteps echoed, and I swallowed nervously. We headed to an elevated dais deep at the back of the hall.

"Yared," the Ibis whispered. When I looked over, she nodded to her left. Meshenitai flanked us, pacing us step for step. Their shotels were partially drawn, the blades glowing. More stood along the walls, each in front of giant carved pillars of stern-faced grown-ups. More royalty? I clenched my teeth. There were enough warriors in this hall alone to help Addis Prime. They had to help. Anger was building inside me. I continued on.

At the far end, in a ring of golden light

cast by several hoverlamps, two giant chairs rested on the floating dais.

This was it, then.

I squared my shoulders and held my chin high. People were depending on me, even if they didn't know it. Addis Prime was depending on me. Haji, Mrs. Marjani, the Ibis's family — they all would suffer if the Werari were left unchecked, free to pillage and destroy. No, this was where it ended. Axum would return to save our homes and defeat the Werari.

"That's far enough." A deep voice spoke, coming from the chair on the left.

Showtime.

The man in the chair leaned forward. The first look I got of him was burning, red-rimmed eyes as he pointed at the Ibis. "Take her."

In an instant, Fatima gripped the Ibis by the arms and carried her off to the side before she could shout or I could go to her aid. A door opened, then closed, and she was swallowed up by darkness. I was on my own, surrounded by dozens of Imperial warriors with their shotels aimed in my direction.

The Emperor turned toward me, the anger twisting his face robbing me of my breath. "Who are you and why have you come here?"

The Emperor of Axum stood and stepped to the edge of the dais. The hovering circle, sensing his movement, lowered and floated forward, until he was only a meter off the floor in front of me. I craned my neck backward. With the light from the lamps bobbing behind his head, the points on his elaborate gold-and-diranium crown looked like spear tips. He was a slim man, and he wore a jump-suit similar to the ones the Ibis and I had put on back at the Ghebbi spaceport. His was gold, however, with a black patch over his heart in the shape of an obelisk with two silver spears crossed behind it. Sharp eyes, brown skin, and a black beard several inches in length that was flecked with gray. Emperor. Negusa.

Father.

And what were his first words in over a decade to his only son?

"I should have you thrown into a ship

and sent back to wherever you came from," he said with a snarl. "Breaking into a restricted area, stealing property of the Axum Empire, and frightening the people!" The tone of his voice shocked me. I took a step back in confusion. Why was he so angry? My words tripped over themselves as I tried to speak, to clarify that I'd come to get their help, to meet them, to return to my family. But I only managed one word.

"I —"

Before I could continue, Captain Leyu's hand was on my shoulder. "Speak only when directed to," she said sternly.

Fury bubbled up inside me, like lava threatening to boil over the side of a volcano.

And shame. My father was . . . rejecting me?

The Emperor returned to his seat, sitting with practiced elegance. The Empress placed a hand on his arm, but her eyes were trained on me as she spoke. "Perhaps, my love, we should divine this intruder's intentions before returning him to the embrace of the stars. Let my Meshenitai escort him to Imperial Security for a . . . debriefing."

Chills went down my spine at the pause before that word. I stood rooted in place, my mind blank and my fingers opening and closing. What was going on? Did they really not know who I was? I reached for my medallion, but my neck was empty. Captain Leyu had it still. I turned to her, but her faceshield was down and her helmet looked straight ahead.

"Captain," I said, hating the pleading note in my voice. "You have to —"

"Silence!" the Emperor thundered. "You were not directed to speak! Enough. Take this miscreant out of my sight. It will be as you say, dear. Have him taken to the interrogation chamber. And inform Auditor Hakim that his . . . expertise . . . is needed."

Audio Transcript File No. 2132.096

Location: [UNDISCLOSED DE-TENTION FACILITY]

Time: 03:30

Subject: Yared [LAST NAME RE-DACTED FOR SECURITY]

Me: And there you have it. That's the whole story — the truth, and nothing but the truth. Next thing I know, I'm in here with your fine company. How's that tea, by the way?

Auditor: It's quite good actually, thank you for — Hey! Enough of the games. You expect me to believe you are the long-lost son of our Imperial highnesses? Preposterous. I've put up with your antics long enough. We will have the truth, one way or another.

Me: Look, I told you everything I know! Why I came, why Addis Prime needs your help . . . If you could just — Hey, what's that?

[muffled noises]

Auditor: This is one of my personal creations. Normal interrogation techniques can be so invasive, even crude.

This is an elegant solution to a thorny problem — extracting information from a subject with minimal damage.

Me: Minimal?

Auditor: Well, nothing is 100 percent.

Me: That's what people who are bad at math say.

Auditor: Perhaps. Let me just slip this over your temples and drop this here like so . . .

Me: Oh, hey, is that your cologne?

Auditor: It is! You like it?

Me: It's incredible.

Auditor: It was a gift, and I just have to find out where it was purchased.

Me: Absolutely. By the way, is this going to hurt?

Auditor: . . . A bit. Now, I just use these controls to begin filtering through your neural patterns. Hmm, it doesn't seem to be . . . Maybe if I . . . No, that didn't work. It's nonresponsive. Who messed with my equipment?

Me: Did you try turning it off and back on again?

Auditor: No, but maybe . . .

Me: Oh, is that a joystick? Try up, down, up, down, quarter turn right. No, your other right. A quarter turn, that was like three whole turns. Wow, you're bad at this. Isn't this your job? Have you never operated a joystick before?

Auditor: This is primitive technology!

Me: But you developed it . . .

Auditor: This is ridiculous. Guards! Take this nuisance back to the holding rooms and wait for my instructions. And send me my assistants. One of them has fiddled with my equipment and I will know who it was. And you . . . do not think you've escaped anything. I will have everything you're hiding. All your secrets. All your lies and mistruths. Take him away!

Me: Thanks for the tea!

CHAPTER FOURTEEN

Auditor Hakim swept out of the room, his face twisted into a scowl and his deep purple demi-cape billowing behind him. A Meshenitai warrior entered the interrogation room once he was gone and untied my restraints. I sat up and rubbed my wrists. The chair I'd been reclined on was flat and hard, and my shoulders and back ached from being forced to remain in that position for . . . actually, I didn't know how much time had passed.

What I did know was that if I couldn't get reinforcements, the Werari would rip right through an unsuspecting and completely unprepared Addis Prime.

"Hey," I said to the Meshenitai, who was raising the chair so I could step off. "Remember when the Emperor said to send me back where I came from? Do you think you could, like, do that now? I'll go home. It's cool. You know what: I should never have come here. I over-stepped my boundaries when I should've respected your personal space. So I'll go! But, also, could you maybe send me back in an exo or two? Or two hundred? I mean, it's not like you all are using them."

"You talk too much." A familiar voice came from the exo's speaker.

I wrinkled my brow. "Fatima?"

"Would you be quiet?"

I resisted as she tried to pull me out the door. "No! Where did you take the Ibis? What did you do with her? If you've hurt her —"

"Oh, for the love of . . . I didn't touch her. I took her to the same place I'm go-ing to take you, *if you would shut your mouth for once in your life!*" She engaged the power armor and stalked out the door. Her grip was like iron around my arm. It was pointless to resist any further. That didn't mean I had to make things easy on her.

"You are such a giant baby," Fatima

snarled as she dragged me down the hall, my body limp as I pretended to snore. Several other guards we passed looked at her strangely, and I grinned. Someone was going to have some interesting questions back at the barracks.

We walked (by which I mean Fatima dragged me) for several minutes, the hubbub of Imperial Security fading as we took one turn, then another, and still another. Finally, boredom set in, and I got to my feet. Fatima glared, pushing me in front of her.

"Walk," she ordered. We traveled downstairs and through a series of hatches, until our way was blocked by a circular hatch with no handle visible anywhere on it.

We stood there for several seconds, but just as I was about to speak, the door hissed and popped open several inches. Fatima pushed it wide, then gestured for me to go in first. I thought about protesting but had probably used up the last of the young Meshenitai's patience with my limp snoring routine.

I stepped into a study. The room was no bigger than a classroom, but soft rugs lined the floor and braided lines of light ran along the vaulted ceilings, casting an orange-pink glow over everything. Several couches and divans encircled a table piled high with fruit. Glasses of fizzing liquid were set about the table, while a small floating brazier warmed a bowl filled with doro wat. The smells of spices and honey and simmering pots of shiro had me nearly drooling.

"Yared!"

I looked over to see the Ibis scramble out of her chair against the far wall. She ran over and hugged me. "You're okay."

"I am," I said, looking around the room. "And here I was thinking you'd been imprisoned in some cell. Is that sambusa?" I stepped by her and picked up a still warm and flaky pastry from a tray. "It is! Ohhhh, this is so good."

"Help yourself," she said sarcastically. "And no, they didn't put me in prison, but they didn't let me talk to anyone. I didn't know what was going on. She said it was for my own protection, but still, I was worried."

I stopped midchew. "She?"

The Ibis's eyes widened. She pointed

to the corner, to a small reclining couch I hadn't noticed before. I'd walked right past it. A woman sat there, partly in shadow, and when she saw us looking, she gathered the folds of her dress and stood.

"My son," said the Empress of Axum.

For the first time in I don't know how long, words failed me. The Empress of Axum stood in front of me, hands smoothing the front of her silver-and-cream dress. She wore a matching head-wrap that neatly bundled her curls. Dangling silver earrings caught the light and held it, like tiny starbursts. Worry lines creased her forehead, and tear tracks marred her gold-dusted brown skin.

She'd been crying.

The Empress took a step forward, then stopped. Her hands flattened, then bunched, then flattened her dress again. She was nervous. The realization jarred me. The Empress. Nervous. She cared as much about this meeting as I did. The whiplash from the interrogation, and my meeting with her and the Emperor, left my brain in a puddle of mush. But there was one thought that rose out of the confusion.

"You are my mother," I said. A statement. A fact. Not a question, but an affirmation.

The Empress nodded and stepped closer.

"I am your son."

She nodded again and closed the distance. We were so close. There was nothing more I wanted to do than to run into her arms, to hug her, to tell her everything about my life that I could remember. She lifted an arm, and her hand, warm and smooth, cupped my cheek. Tears pricked the corner of my eyes.

And that's why my next question felt like I was ripping my own heart out.

"So why didn't you want me?"

Her hand froze as my voice broke. All the hurt I kept inside a lockbox of bravado had broken free. The lonely nights. The days I'd wanted someone to hold me, to promise me safety, to be with me. The tears that had been threatening to spill now fell freely. Several splashed on her hand, but the Empress — my mother — didn't move. Instead, she pulled me into a fierce hug.

Sobs racked my body as the woman who I'd searched for desperately, the person I'd dreamed about meeting, held me. I'd had a thousand fantasies about yelling at her, about dismissing her. I didn't need her! I'd made it; look at me now; look at what I made of myself.

Look at me now . . .

This was what a mother's hug felt like. Security. Reassurance. Strength.

"My baby," she whispered into my hair. "My boy, my son, my lion. I love you so much. We *never* wanted to part with you, but it's how we ensured your safety." She knelt, both hands on my shoulders, and I saw she was crying, too. We had the same eyes, big and brown and full of tears. "Sending you away was the hardest thing I've ever had to do. Not a day went by that I didn't stare at the stars and call your name. It ate at my very soul, but losing you meant you were safe. That you would be able to grow up and shine, my prince! My heart! And look at you. I cannot tell you how proud I am. Seeing your face has made these years worth it. My boy has returned to me. Negusa Nagast, O kings of kings, smile on your family, your son has returned."

Slowly, my arms encircled her, and we hugged each other as we cried.

Mother and son.

Finally, she pulled away. Sniffing, she wiped her eyes, then smiled as the Ibis handed her a tissue. "Thank you, dear. And thank you for standing by my son when we were unable to. Axum is only as strong as its children, and I think we will be just fine." The Ibis blushed but came to stand by my side.

The Empress moved quickly to Fatima, who handed her a silk-wrapped bundle.

"I have so many questions," I said, wiping my face with the back of my arm.

"I know, but time is of the essence. We are watched constantly."

The Ibis and I exchanged looks. "The Werari," I said.

The Empress nodded. She approached, unfolding the silk and holding it out. On it rested my medallion and two long curved daggers, the likes of which I'd never seen. They reminded me of the shotels the Meshenitai carried. Polished black handles were inlaid with a familiar icon — the obelisk with two crossed spears behind it. They rested inside braided silver sheathes, decorated with ornate designs and metalwork. Fatima took them as the Empress draped the medallion over my head and tucked it beneath my shirt.

"Listen, my son," she said, her voice low and rhythmic. "This is a story I have long practiced but never recited. Now, when I have so much I want to say to you and so many things I want to learn about you, time prevents me. I am forced to tell this bit of history instead. Ten years ago, the invaders came. The land-eaters. The devourers. The Werari. Thwarted once before, they returned with their monster, the Bulgu. Greed and jealousy drove them. Their goal was the key to Axum's spread across the galaxy. If they discovered it, they would be able to sow their seeds of hatred and destruction throughout the stars. Axum, and the free worlds in and out of the Empire, would end as we knew it.

"But what the invaders didn't know was that after their first attempt, a plan was hatched to protect the key. It was encoded, and all knowledge of it destroyed, except for one last copy that was hidden in the heart of Axum." The Empress tapped my chest. I nodded to show I understood. My blood. "The key was then entrusted to one of the Empire's greatest heroes, a man who lived for the survival of Axum. That man shouldered a great lie, cloaking himself in it so that the truth would remain hidden. Our greatest hero became a villain."

General Moti Berihun. He *wasn't* a traitor. He'd only pretended to be, so that suspicion wouldn't fall on him. Just like he'd pretended to be my uncle to keep me safe.

And I'd called him a stranger. Shame burned through me.

My mother lifted my chin, as if she suspected what I was thinking. "The shadow of that lie," she said slowly, "covers us all. But now we come to the fulcrum. On one side is the free world, and on the other, the Werari. Even now your father distracts them."

"They're here?" the Ibis asked.

The Empress nodded.

"So," I said slowly, "he doesn't hate me?"

Her eyes softened, and she hugged me again. "Your father loves you very much," she said, her voice thick. "It eats him inside that your first meeting unfolded as such. But do not doubt his love. Never doubt! The great lie was a terrible necessity, and we will answer for it, but for now it must hold. Just for a while longer."

I swallowed. "What do we do?"

She held up one of the daggers. "The ship you arrived on is still powered and ready to fly. Your Guardian is on board. The two of you must fly back to Addis Prime and find the man who wears the lie. You both must show him your jilé and tell him the fires must burn again."

"That's it? Just the two of us? What about Fatima?"

The Empress shook her head. "Every Meshenitai will be needed here. The Werari will not be stalled with half-truths for much longer."

Fatima looked at my mother. "It's time,

Your Highness. They must leave now."

"Wait," I said. "We just got here! How can we do this by ourselves? We're kids! We don't have power armor or glowing swords. We're not warriors."

"Never say that!" my mother said. She kissed my forehead, then drew me and the Ibis into a hug, pulling us both close. "Armor doesn't make the warrior, my son. Heart does. Now go. Fatima will guide you most of the way, and then you must flee!"

I nodded, emotions roiling inside me. The Ibis and I each took a jilé. We gasped when blue lines rippled out as our fingers touched the black handles. They vibrated in our palms, then fell still. Fatima showed us how the sheath adhered to a special spot on the jumpsuits we wore.

"Only draw these to defend yourself or others," she warned. We nodded.

The Empress smoothed her dress, and Fatima reapplied gold dust to her cheeks. When they were ready, the Meshenitai moved to the door, looked at us all, and then opened it —

— to see white-helmeted Werari aiming

304

their corrupted shotels at her.

A man stepped into the room, and my heart plummeted.

"Well, well, Your Highness," Captain Ascar said, his hands clasped behind his back. Alarms began to blare inside the Empress's chamber. "Someone has been keeping secrets."

CHAPTER FIFTEEN

Eight Werari troopers crowded into the room. They surrounded us — one Meshenitai, an Empress, and two kids. The odds weren't exactly in our favor. Apparently my mother didn't share the same view.

"Captain Ascar," she said. The smile on her face was cold, not quite reaching her eyes. "They let the dog off his leash."

The Werari leader removed his helmet and rubbed a hand through his close-cropped hair. His golden eyes swept the room. He smirked when they landed on me. I glared back at him, but he'd already returned to my mother.

"Now, now, Empress — I would watch that tongue. It'd be a shame if something were to happen to you . . . or your son."

My mother's eyes widened. Just a bit,

but the Werari captain didn't miss anything. His cruel smirk grew even crueler. "Yes," he hissed. "To think we had the power of Axum right in front of us and nearly smothered it. For once, I'm *glad* someone in my unit was incompetent." He didn't turn around, but one of the troopers behind him shuffled. It was the soldier who carried the scanling on her back.

"Now," Captain Ascar continued. "Let me make this absolutely clear. You, my Empress of Axum, will hand over everything to do with the Menelik drives, including the key, the algorithm for decoding it, and all the astrogation data associated with it. If you do not . . ." He nodded, and two troopers leapt forward, grabbing me and the Ibis and dragging us back behind the captain. "Well, let's just say your reunion will be . . . cut short."

The sounds of metal weapons being drawn filled the room.

Frustration filled me, and I clenched my fists. It wasn't fair. I'd finally found my parents, connected with my mother, and learned how much Uncle Moti had sacrificed to protect me and Axum. And then here came the world's worst party crashers, dragging down the vibe.

"Yared, don't." The Ibis was watching me. Was I that obvious?

When you can't run away, run off at the mouth. That's what I always said.

"Yared —"

"You know what you fine specimens of discipline need?" I said loudly. Really loudly. Basically shouting. "A flag. Something that says, 'We couldn't contribute to society, so we decided to destroy it.' Maybe in a nice taupe color." I leaned to the soldier next to me. "Do you like taupe?"

Captain Ascar turned around, his lips pressed thin. "Like mother like son. If he speaks again, gag him."

"So the funny thing about that is," I continued, "taupe isn't for everyone. It's a bland color. You all look like you'd be fans of a dingy off-white flag. Something that shouts, 'I have no culture of my own, so let me steal it.' "

"Yared," the Ibis whispered. "Do you know what you're doing?"

I grinned at her as Captain Ascar stalked toward us and patted the bulky compartment on my waist. "Nope! I'm flying by the seat of my pants." I winked, and she stared at me before her face fell and she groaned. My plans inspire awe, what can I say?

I turned my attention back to the leader of the Werari. I had to time this just right. Too soon, and we wouldn't be able to escape. Too late and . . . well, I didn't want to think about what would happen if I was too late.

The Empress and Fatima were staring as if I was babbling incoherently. It probably sounded that way to them. I tried to project confidence, to send a look that said, *Trust me, I've got this.* But Captain Ascar stepped in front of me. He pulled a strip of cloth from his pocket.

"I warned you," he said.

"That's funny." I edged backward, just enough so I could see my mother. "My uncle used to warn me, too. He'd say the same thing every time I got in trouble at school for talking back. Funny thing is, he said my father used to say the same thing to *him* when they were growing up."

The Empress's eyes widened.

I winked and continued. "It goes, if you're always running your mouth, one day it's going to run you off a cliff without a *parachute*!"

I slammed the emergency release catch on the jumpsuit, and the Ibis did the same on her suit at the same time. Parachute foam sprayed out in an arc, catching the unsuspecting Werari around the arms and waist. As the foam hardened, several of the soldiers fell, knocked into the others. Soon the room was full of shouts and confusion.

I couldn't help it — I started snickering.

A hand grabbed my shoulder and spun me around. It was Captain Ascar. Foam had hardened on the left side of his face, giving him a horrifying expression. His eyes were full of rage. He held the Ibis with his other hand, and glared back and forth between us, his voice a hiss of fury.

"Enough games!"

Blue light speared the air. The captain yelped as he stumbled back and released us. The Empress stood in the middle of the room, a lightspear in each hand. Fatima crouched at her side, shotel drawn. "Run, children!" my mother called. "You know what you must do."

"Come with us!" I shouted.

She shook her head as more Werari soldiers began to free themselves of the foam, climbing to their feet. "My battle is here."

Captain Ascar moved forward, a sneer on his face as he cradled his right wrist. "You are risking my ire, Your Highness."

The lance tip flicked out, smashing into a soldier trying to creep around her. He tumbled to the ground with a cry of pain. The Empress settled into a crouch with a smile. "The wild dog barks and barks as it tries to stay clear of the lion. Come, dog. Let me hear you yelp. Fatima!"

Fatima's thrusters flared, sending her forward at a dash. She flashed by the captain and scooped the Ibis and me up in her arms. Fatima skidded to a stop by the door, hurled us out, and slid up her faceshield.

"Run," she said, before slamming the controls on the inner wall.

The hatch closed.

We sprinted through Axum's corridors. I followed the Ibis without thought, turning when she did, climbing ladders she pointed to, even leaping through an anti-grav agrarium to reach a service tunnel on the other side. I nearly became tangled in an aggressive floating pod of synthetic algae, if not for the Ibis snatching me away at the last second.

"Nearly there," she continued to say, over and over, as much for her as for me.

And yet I still couldn't think about the present, let alone the future. The only thing turning over in my mind was the look on my mother's face as Fatima shoved the Ibis and I out the door. Pride and fear. Anxiety and happiness. And anger. Lots of anger. Was that strange blend of emotions a common expression for mothers to make? For all parents? I'd only just met her — learned who she was, how her hugs felt, what her pride did to my soul — and now we were separated again. It wasn't fair. It wasn't FAIR!

"Yared?"

I looked up. The Ibis stood several

meters away. I'd stopped running.

"Yared, come on," she said. "I need your help."

"We left her," I mumbled.

The Ibis hurried back to me and took my hand. "We had to leave. She's distracting the Werari so we can find General Moti. If we don't escape, she'll have risked her life for nothing. Is that what you want?"

The urgency in her voice penetrated the fog surrounding my thoughts. I looked into her eyes, then shook my head.

"Of course not," she said. "Now help me get this thing to take us back to our ship."

I finally noticed the spinning pyramid that floated just behind the Ibis. A station guide. Blue light covered it as it spun, like an aura or forcefield. I stepped forward.

"Selam, Your Highness. The space station Axum is currently under a state of emergency. Access to certain locations is limited, as is the functionality of this guide. How may I be of service?"

My mother. Lightspears in her arms,

surrounded by Werari.

Addis Prime, waking to violence and bloodshed.

The hardest thing I ever had to do was my duty, Uncle Moti had said.

"Yared," the Ibis said softly.

I had to do my duty. If that meant being separated from my parents for a little while longer, then that's what it took. My mother and father sent me, their only son, away to protect both me and the nation they loved. My uncle — yes, I could say it now without feeling like it wasn't true — accepted the label of traitor to protect the nation he loved. If they could do all that, then I could do something difficult for my nation as well.

"Take me to the scout ship *Ezana,*" I said, proud of how my voice didn't shake. "And chart a course to Addis Prime."

"Okay, so I've got good news and I've got bad news."

I grunted.

"Which one do you want first?" the Ibis asked.

I shifted my feet slightly and grunted.

"What does that mean?" she asked.

"It means," I said, squeezing the words through gritted teeth, "that your boots are digging into my neck. If you don't hurry, we're both going to have some bad news called gravity."

We stood in one of Axum's many service tunnels. Well, I stood in the tunnel and the Ibis stood on top of me, peeking out of a maintenance hatch into the docking ring where the people mover that would carry us to the *Ezana* waited. I'd remembered Captain Leyu mentioning the tunnels — grid-like charcoal-gray passages that ran in between the decks. They allowed techs to work on different sections of the enormous space station without impacting day-to-day activities. After several requests, whispered threats, and a few princely authoritative overrides, I'd managed to get the spinning pyramid guide to lead us on a longer route that avoided the main corridors where the Werari were sure to be lurking. Instead, we traveled beneath many of the abandoned residential sections. I tried not to think of the empty streets and homes, once filled with shrieking and laughing children and their bemused parents. The silence weighed on me, insisting I do something. Fix it. Give the displaced a home.

"I will," I promised, my voice a whisper.

"What?" The Ibis tapped my shoulder with the toe of her boot. I squatted, letting her step down onto my thigh and then hop to the ground. "Did you say something?"

I shook my head. "It's nothing. Give me the good news."

She blew out a puff of air. "Well, according to the status screen up there, the ship isn't guarded. There's no movement in the tunnels, either."

"Oh. Oh! That's good, right?" Her face was grim, and I frowned. "Right?"

"Sort of. There aren't any guards *yet*, but as soon as we step foot out there, there will be. And then *those* guards will call the reinforcements."

"Wait, what reinforcements?"

The Ibis hesitated, then sighed. "The ones that haven't landed yet. That's the rest of the bad news. More Werari will be here soon. The status screen *also* says there are four troop transports inbound. They're heading toward where the *Ezana* is docked, blocking our flight path."

I stared at the Ibis, wrestling with the numbers in my head. "Four transports. That's . . . two hundred troopers. The Meshenitai will be overwhelmed!"

"I know." She hesitated and then hurriedly dropped the rest of the bad news. Honestly, she had a talent for this. I was impressed. "But that's not enough troop carriers."

"What do you mean not enough? Two hundred is plenty!"

"No, you don't understand. Dropships don't fly solo —"

"They're transported on carriers," I said, finishing her sentence.

"Exactly." She chewed her lip nervously. "That carrier is probably in a holding pattern out of sight. Four transports is nothing. Standard carriers hold up to twenty-five, and I don't know why the Werari's would be any different. Either they're holding forces back somewhere, or they're planning on landing them somewhere else."

She didn't specify where, but I'd known what she was leading up to before she even finished the sentence. Addis Prime. If the Werari got their thieving hands on the Gebeya and the Menelik drives, they would have nearly everything they needed to spread across the galaxy. I couldn't let that happen. But I also couldn't just leave my parents here by themselves, under siege by Captain Ashy and his crew. I had to distract them, give the Meshenitai a chance to get the few remaining people of Axum to safety.

It was time to be proactive, not reactive.

"Okay," I said, pacing. "Let's break it down. The Meshenitai and my parents are trapped by the Werari on board the station. More Werari are coming. And even more are probably heading to Addis Prime. Somehow we have to stop them, while also sending my parents backup."

I stopped pacing. The Ibis met my eyes. Her expression mirrored my own.

"We need reinforcements," we both said at the same time.

■ ■ ■ ■

I climbed up into the docking ring and ran over to the people mover. The Ibis lay crouched on the bottom, her head peeking over the side as she kept watch. She shot me a questioning look when I slipped over the railing and scooted to her side.

"Did you get it?"

I nodded. "No thanks to that ridiculous guide. I swear, my first proclamation as prince will be to ban all spinning, floating pyramids from Axum territories."

"Oh, you're making proclamations now?"

I shrugged. "Maybe a suggestion, then. Even a prayer. Something. Anyway, I've got them." I handed the Ibis a small vidscreen. She scrolled through the long lists of characters on it, then nodded.

"Perfect." She started to say something, then paused. "You know, once we start, everyone on the station is going to know where we are. They'll come for us. We'll have ten minutes, maybe less, to get to the *Ezana.* Are you sure you want to do this? Maybe the Meshenitai can hold."

I shook my head. "Maybe isn't good enough. Let's get them some reinforcements, then go save Addis Prime."

The Ibis nodded. Without another word, she popped off a panel beneath the controls. I kept a watch out as she worked, rerouting wires and uploading new info into the people movers' systems. After a few minutes, she popped the panel back into place and sat up. She handed me the vidscreen, several wires clipped to it. "Ready?"

I took a deep breath, then nodded.

The Ibis activated the people mover, and pushed the throttle forward. "Here goes nothing."

We lurched forward, heading in the opposite direction of where the *Ezana* waited. I know, it seemed counterproductive, but that was the idea. Hopefully we had the element of surprise . . .

"First stop, Yared," the Ibis called back to me. We were steadily picking up speed, so her words were nearly drowned out by the air rushing past us. I angled myself for stability, then eyed the upcoming traversal zone. Another residential section. I really, really hoped this worked.

Instead of slowing down, we blew past. I tapped a command, and instead of the normal announcement, the alert codes I'd had the guide bot provide me (after extensive threats) blared out of the people mover's speakers.

"Alert, alert. This is a priority-one alert! On the orders of the Imperial Family, a priority-one alert has been called. Please clear the area. Again, a priority-one alert has been called on the orders of the Imperial Family."

The people mover continued to pick up speed, which was a good thing, as the Ibis was shouting in frustration.

"What is it?"

She pointed behind us. I turned, then groaned. A half-dozen Werari exos raced after us, their leg thrusters spouting blue-white flames as they closed the distance between us. They were still several hundred meters behind, but the people mover wasn't built for speed. It was only a matter of time before the troopers were right behind us.

A flash of silver caught my eye off to

the right. Could it be? I squinted, then grinned. Three more silver bolts zigged and zagged around obstacles as they kept pace, and I thought I spotted two on the left.

"Don't worry about the Werari," I said, turning around and pointing toward the next traversal zone. "I've got some friends on the way."

I'd learned this from Uncle Moti. In an emergency situation, like the time I got lost in New Oromia as a kid, all security units go on high alert. Priority one meant the main objective of all security units was to search out and secure Imperial Family members. And did you know that Guardians were considered security units? That's how Besa found me, even though I hadn't been linked with her yet. And that meant any second now . . .

A loud roar filled the ring, followed by another, and another.

"Almost there, Yared!" the Ibis shouted.

I raised my hand, judging the distance. The Werari would be on us as soon as we stopped, but maybe, just maybe . . .

The people mover sped around a bend.

Suddenly, the docking pad for the *Ezana* was rapidly approaching. I jerked my hand down, and the Ibis engaged the vehicles brakes. A loud humming sounded as the antigrav system reversed, jerking us to a stop so abrupt I nearly fell backward.

I jumped off, and the Ibis followed. We raced to the large oval hatch. The *Ezana* shimmered on the screens surrounding it, so close and yet so far. I felt the corridor floor rumbling as the Werari thundered toward us. This was it. We had no weapons, the warbow and lightspear having been confiscated by Captain Leyu. Was this the time to use the jilé? No, I had to focus on running. Maybe we could make it. If I'd gotten the timing even a second off —

We reached the hatch and turned. The Werari were right behind us, light glimmering off their helmets and the tips of their stolen shotels. There was no outrunning them. I grabbed the Ibis's hand. We stood, shoulder to shoulder. Thirty meters. Twenty. Ten. Five.

The tip of the leading Werari's shotel was seconds away from creating a Yared kebab, when claws the size of a hand ripped it in half. I grinned, sidestepping the broken weapon as it tumbled past me down the corridor. "Why don't you all pick on someone your own size?" I shouted.

The Werari turned to face twelve fully armored Guardians prowling toward them. Robotic lions far larger than me rumbled warnings in their throats. Some had flowing silver manes with sparks rippling up and down the metallic strands. Others were lionesses like my Besa, with ridged spikes guarding their spine and flanks.

"Retreat!" one of the Werari shouted. Then he backed up into a Guardian, which batted him aside like a cat would a mouse. That broke the spirit of the rest of the troopers. They fled, and the Guardians gave chase. Or most of them did. One lioness broke away from the pack.

I let out a wordless shout and dropped to my knees as Besa pounced on me. She nuzzled my face and grunted as I hugged her neck, ignoring how much the spines hurt. We were reunited. My Besa. My lioness. My Guardian.

The Ibis cleared her throat. When I looked over, she nodded at the hatch, behind which the *Ezana* waited. "You two can exchange pleasantries *after* we're safely aboard." Besa padded over and nuzzled her. The Ibis rolled her eyes but scratched the lioness behind the ears. "Yes, I missed you, too. Now, Yared, if you're not too busy?"

"Well, I kind of wanted to see the Guardians go to work on the Werari . . ." I let the sentence trail off at the glint in the Ibis's eye. I quickly pressed the medallion my mother had given me into the slot on Besa's forehead. The hatch unlocked — the Guardian Protocol superseded all other commands — and we ran onto the ship.

"Where are you going?" I asked the Ibis as she began to sit down next to me. I pointed at the flight deck. "Someone has to pilot this thing, and we all know I'm useless at that. Unless you want another skysail incident."

The Ibis gawked, then threw her arms around my neck. "Thank you," she whispered.

"Just get us there in one piece," I said.

She smacked me gently and sprinted to the flight deck. Before she was finished strapping into her harness, she'd already expanded the screens and called up launch protocols. I secured Besa, then myself, and took a deep breath. Axum wasn't in the clear yet, but with the Guardians' assistance, my parents and the Meshenitai would have an edge against the Werari. Now all we had to do was —

The call screen flashed, and then the cruel face of Captain Ascar peered down at us all. "You insolent brats," he snarled. "You think your little stunt did anything? You've only delayed the inevitable. I will have the key, and soon."

"You're finished!" I shouted. "Your troopers are running with their tails between their legs."

"Oh, I have plenty more to spare," the Werari captain said. His leaned forward so his face filled the screen, his sneer looming over us. "Still, why waste them on *you*? Instead, I think I'll send an old friend of yours. See you soon . . . young prince."

His face disappeared without any other

explanation. It didn't matter. The Ibis had already figured it out.

"Oh no. Oh no, no, no. Yared . . . I found the carrier. It's heading back to Addis Prime and it just launched something into the atmosphere."

"What? More troop shuttles?"

"No. Look." She brought up the object on the giant screen. It was glowing red-hot, large and oblong, with a familiar ax-shaped head knifing through the sky.

The Bulgu.

CHAPTER SIXTEEN

The *Ezana* raced down to Addis Prime. A heavy, dreadful silence filled the flight deck inside. The Ibis stared at the controls and bit her fingernails, talking softly with the ship's Zenaye system to make slight course corrections. She was trying to coax every bit of speed from the engines that she could. Me? I glowered at the screen floating in the middle of the ship, which showed the streamlined shape of the Bulgu barreling toward Addis Prime.

We had to get there in time. We just had to. No one was prepared to defend against the monster's return. I remembered the damage it did last time, when it was just looking for me. What could it do if it went on an indiscriminate rampage? Who would be hurt? Whose homes would be lost?

The Ibis and her family's orbital farm flashed in my mind. All her sisters, her parents — the Bulgu was more than capable of tearing their home apart in moments. And the rest of Addis Prime. The people, the families, the businesses, the schools, the Gebeya. All of it was in danger!

"Childrennnnnn," a voice sang creepily through the ship's comms. "Oh, little childreeeennnnn."

The image of the Bulgu disappeared. Every screen in the ship flickered, and then the golden eyes of Captain Ascar reappeared, staring down at us like a wraith.

"Ah, there you are," he said. "Fleeing. Typical. I should have known. Your famed General Moti did the same, if I'm not mistaken. At the moment when he could have spared countless lives, he chose to run. And now you're doing the same. But there's still time to save Addis Prime. Turn around. Face me. Show me you're a fighter, and I promise no one else needs to get hurt. Prove to me you have what it takes to be a leader, and this entire world will be safe. I can still call off the attack. You just. Need. To face me."

"Ignore him, Yared," the Ibis whispered from the flight deck. "He's trying to get you to do something foolish."

My right palm rested on Besa's back. My lioness stood in her harness, her eyes watching me, her presence giving me strength. Was it true? No one needed to get hurt?

I hesitated to answer.

"Yared?" the Ibis called.

"I know," I whispered. "Keep going."

"Fine. Listen to your little friend, *Yared,*" Captain Ascar said, his tone mocking in a way that grated on me. I wanted to do nothing more than to turn the ship around and fire arrow after arrow from a warbow into his face. "Don't do anything *foolish,*" he continued. "Save yourself. Run. Hide. Fly away. Live in fear for the rest of your life, scrounging and skulking in the shadows. A nothing. A nobody. Just like old man Moti."

SNAP.

The handheld screen cracked beneath my palms. I stared at it, the fractured display now frozen with the image of the Bulgu piercing through the Authority Net. Blue lightning rippled across its ax head. A single, red-rimmed eye stared down at what I imagined was the sprawling, honeycomb districts of Addis Prime.

"Fly away, Yared."

Is this how Uncle Moti felt when he left with me? Like he'd abandoned everyone he cared about? Like a coward? A failure? My parents were back in Axum. My parents! Everything I'd ever worked for in my life had been to have a family, to be recognized by them, to shout my name proudly from the tops of the highlands.

"Run away, Yared. Run."

But I had family on Addis Prime, too. Uncle Moti. Maybe he wasn't related by blood, but he was related by choice. I *chose* to call him Uncle. And if going through battles and struggles and hard times with someone made them as close to you as siblings could be, then I *chose* the Ibis as my sister. Kamali, Haji, even the Toe Twins . . . they were all my family, too. Because Addis Prime was my house, and the Werari were trying to take it from me.

I could not let that happen. I couldn't run away.

I looked up at the giant image of Captain Ascar and blew an extended, longer-than-five-seconds raspberry at him. "Sorry, I wish I could help. But I have one more level to beat and a personal record to set. Do me a favor, though, okay? Say hi to the rest of the Guardians."

His face scrunched into a furious expression. "What Guardians, you insolent little worm? I will —"

A roar interrupted him. I couldn't help it — I giggled. But you should have seen his expression. All serious and evil, and then it twisted to horror like he just smelled something nasty. It was perfect.

"Toodles!" I said, wiggling my fingers at him. I nodded at the Ibis, and she cut the feed.

She grinned at me. "You had me worried there. That's normally the time when you decide to go all one-boy-show and take on everyone at the same time."

"Not this time." I tossed the broken

screen to the side, taking one last look at the face of the Bulgu. Then I brought up my workstation screen and furiously typed in some commands. "We're going to need help for this fight. It's time to call for our own backup."

Every screen in Addis Prime flickered, then went black. All of them. The ones centered in the torsos of the bunamechs. The giant ones in each classroom in every school in Addis Prime. The giant tower in New Oromia, in the financial district, in the highland factories — all the screens in the entire region cut away from their feeds. In their place, one boy in a sleek black jumpsuit and a black-and-gold lion's mask stood on the bridge of a spaceship. On his left side sat an armored lion, and on his right, a tall girl with coiled hair wearing a similar jumpsuit and a gleaming silver bird mask.

A graphic appeared above the boy's head.

YARED THEGR8, LVL 94

And above the girl's head:

THE IBIS, LVL 96

The lioness had her own graphic proclaiming her a level 42 familiar. The three of them remained silent, until finally, after nearly a minute had passed, the boy began to speak.

"Citizens of Addis Prime. Some of you might recognize my screen name. Others might know my face and who I was supposed to be. I ask that you forgive me for interrupting your feeds, but time is short and our future is at stake.

"Death is coming. By the end of this message, it may have already arrived. A robotic creature called the Bulgu has been sent to terrorize Addis Prime. It was sent by a group of people called the Werari, and they're coming.

"I know what you all are thinking — it can't be true. This is a hoax. I get it. I thought the same thing. But I've been there. I've seen it, and I've seen the Werari. You have to believe me."

The boy took a deep breath.

"But I know it will take more than faith to convince you. So I come to you not only as a citizen of Addis Prime, but as a prince of Axum."

The boy removed the mask, and the graphic above his head disappeared. Instead, a giant swirling cloud of golden pix-elated dust swept up and around him, covering him on-screen with a sparkling outline from head to toe. A new graphic appeared, one generated by the Authority system, not HKO. An official title.

YARED I, PRINCE OF AXUM

The boy stepped forward, until his face filled the entire screen. The expression he wore was haunted, yet determined.

"The Werari are coming. The Bulgu is coming. But I am coming, too, and together we can stop them once and for all. So I ask you, Addis Prime. Play a level in the Hunt for Kaleb's Obelisk with me. Meet me at the Gebeya, where we will push the invaders out. Please. This time we must choose a side, because in this round? We're playing for keeps."

The signal cut out, and every screen went black.

High above the Gebeya, a glowing streak split the sky, crashing to the earth with a thunderous explosion of sound and rubble.

The Bulgu had returned.

The red light on the top of the spinning guide turned off, and I sighed, dropping into a crouch next to Besa. "At least that thing is good for something. Do you think everyone got the message?"

The Ibis was already pulling off her mask and returning to the flight deck, where she collapsed into the chair and threw up a vidscreen filled with multiple subwindows, each with a different feed. She studied them, discarding a couple that didn't show what she wanted. A fierce grin crossed her face. "All the social hubs are *blazing.* Everybody's talking about you, or the Werari, or . . . oh. Oh no." She looked up at me. "Or the Bulgu."

"It's here?" I moved quickly to her side, Besa right behind me.

The Ibis pointed at several feeds. "Apparently it crashed down on the north side of the market district, not far from the Gebeya. The good news is that all the feeds are filling up with pictures of it, so everyone knows what you said was true. The bad news is . . . well, it's the Bulgu."

Pictures quickly cycled through all the feeds. In one, the ax-headed creature smashed a hovercan. In another, it obliterated a home. There were several shots of it looking up as orbital farms floated by overhead, and the Ibis tensed. I dropped a hand on her shoulder.

"Don't worry. This time, it's going down." Then, to the Zenaye AI system, I started calling out commands. "*Ezana,* bring up a map of the area and identify the hostile bionic as the Bulgu."

The main screen above the flight deck rippled, and a new image appeared. It was a three-dimensional holomap of Addis Prime. A red icon flashed a short distance away from the giant floating sphere representing the Gebeya. I grimaced. "Show the Bulgu's previous path."

A glowing trail appeared, starting in the center of one of the residential kebeles and leading south. "It's heading straight for the Gebeya. The Werari want those Menelik drives, and they don't care who gets trampled or hurt on the way."

The Ibis checked her screens. "Two minutes until we reach the Gebeya. I really hope you have a plan."

I sighed. "I do. I just need Uncle Moti. Hopefully he saw the broadcast. If he and Kamali can distract the Bulgu, I can power up the Menelik drives and send it to Axum. Once the station is restored to its full capabilities, it's over for the Werari. I need everyone's help."

"Whaaaat? Yared the Great, asking for assistance?"

I brushed an imaginary speck of dust from my jumpsuit. "Sometimes even the greats require a hand now and then." Besa shouldered my legs, and I grinned. "Yes, you help me all the time."

The *Ezana* flew over Addis Prime, its thrusters sending clouds of exhaust and dust whipping around as it slowed to hover over the south side of the giant floating market. The Ibis linked the Zenaye system to her comms and put the ship on autopilot. We dropped onto a drone docking pad, and she sent the ship up on a preprogrammed flight pattern, then studied her comms.

"Okay, we're good. The *Ezana* will send me updates on the Bulgu's movements and any other hostile force. But we've got to find your uncle fast. It's closing in on us."

We raced into the Gebeya, Besa leading the way. I trusted her navigation system more than my memory, and we didn't have time to waste. The damage from the last attack still remained. It was a reminder of what could happen again very soon to the rest of Addis Prime. Clothes were strewn about, dangling from partially collapsed stalls or in piles on the floor. Vegetables squished beneath our feet as we ran deeper and deeper into the darkness, zigzagging around blocked aisles and hopping over overturned crates. One stall that sold memory chips for archival purposes still smoked. I winced at the giant solidified mountain of circuits and plastic. That was someone's life savings, destroyed.

And it was empty. So empty.

"Yared, I don't like the look of this . . ." the Ibis began.

"We can do it," I said, putting as much conviction into my voice as possible. I didn't know if that was for her, or for the doubt swirling around inside *me.*

She looked at me as we sprinted down

a wide corridor, but before she could say anything, Besa stopped and pawed at a section of the wall. We skidded to a stop, and I pressed my palm flat against the hidden biometric scanner. "Authorize, Prince Yared of Axum."

A crack appeared with a hiss, and then the section of wall rotated inward. I smiled. Thank goodness for Besa. I would've never remembered the way into Uncle Moti and Kamali's hideout. We ran through the tunnel and entered the hideout.

"Uncle Moti!" I shouted. "Kamali?"

But the room was dark and empty.

Something beeped once, then again. I ignored it, too stunned to pay attention. I'd been sure Uncle Moti would be here. How else would he plan the defense of Addis Prime? Where would he go? He couldn't have left, could he?

The sneering face of Captain Ascar appeared in my mind, just for an instant, and I squeezed my eyes shut to help rid myself of the image, but his words lingered in my ear.

He fled, like a coward . . .

Something beeped again. The Ibis groaned. When I turned around, she held up her wrist and showed me her comms screen. "It's here. Not only that, but seven Werari troop transports just dropped through the Authority Net."

I gawked. "Seven?" I stared at the different workstations, frustration mounting. We had to power up the Menelik drives, and now. "Okay, here's what we're going to do. Can you set up an uplink and route it through the *Ezana*?"

"Of course. What are you going to do?"

"Unite our home." I was already heading to the large central workstation. Besa followed me, and I pulled the medallion from her chest and set it on the flat screen in the middle of the station. Light appeared, multicolored rays that raced to the medallion, swirling around it as the workstation powered up.

A holo-display appeared above the medallion. I stared in amazement as the Ibis joined me. "Is that Axum?"

The space station materialized out of light, in its full configuration. The entire obelisk, surrounded by all three docking rings and the giant Menelik drives —

minus the thousands of shops from the Gebeya — attached at the bottom. Then, one by one, the missing sections became highlighted in red. Their names appeared in a list at the bottom, each with a sliding toggle next to it with the caption REENGAGE?

I tried the other ring sections first, sliding the toggle to the right to see what would happen, but each time the screen flashed. "UNABLE TO SIGNAL REMOTE ENGAGE," the system read. "MANUAL RECOVERY REQUIRED." A series of astrogation coordinates appeared next to each ring section.

The Ibis frowned. "The space station is going to have to jump to wherever those coordinates represent. I've never seen those on a map."

"No," I said softly. "They would've erased them."

"Who?"

"Axum. My parents. So no one could find the other sections. That's why Axum was so empty — they loaded everyone on the other ring sections to keep them safe and dropped them at those coordinates, intending to come back for them."

Except they never did, because they had to hide the Menelik drives so the Werari couldn't get them. The people of Axum had been cut off from their home, their nation, for nearly a decade, unable to return. Until now. My finger trembled as I slowly touched the toggle for the Menelik drives . . . the engines idling beneath our feet. I slid it to the right, holding it for just a second before letting go.

The screen flashed . . . green.

"REENGAGING THRUSTER MODULE WITH MAIN STATION," the system read. "STAND BY."

The entire room began to rumble. A fierce joy swept through me. Just then, the weird beeping intensified, and Besa pawed at my wrist. "Mrowr."

"What?" I looked down, then did a double take. My wrist comm was flashing. I activated it and watched — first in shock, then in delight — as message after message poured in, both on my private feed and in public forums.

"What is it?" the Ibis asked.

A fierce grin crossed my face as I looked at her. "They're coming. The other HKO squads. They're coming to help."

She let out a whoop but froze when her comms unit also began to beep. An image rose into the air above it.

The Bulgu had arrived.

BOOM.

The cargo ship docking pad shook as we stepped outside. Below us, the Bulgu slammed its head into the underside of the Gebeya. "It's trying to get at the Menelik drives!" I shouted. Besa yowled in distress, and I held on to her with one hand. "We have to give them time to power up. If that giant can opener damages one more engine, this whole market will crash."

A thrum caught my attention, and the Ibis pointed up into the sky. "Look!"

The air above us filled with vessels of all shapes and sizes. There were skysails like the one the Ibis piloted, and the smaller moonsail variations, which could only fit one person. Giant old delivery drones converted to haul teff now held shouting kids. Haji rode in one, piloting his transport and pulling a series of his hacked drones behind him. He pumped his fist at me, and I saluted him. Even the Toes had come, though how they'd shoved themselves into an old battered skysail was beyond me.

I turned to the Ibis. "You ready?" I asked. "We're going to have to do this the hard way."

"Lead the way . . . my prince," she said, keying in a command to recall the *Ezana.* I stuck my tongue out at her. The ship swooped down to the pad, and we hopped aboard. "You call out the formations; I'll get us into position."

I sat at a station, and Besa stood beside me. Using the ship's comms, I connected to the hub of HKO. Dozens and dozens of icons winked into existence above the station. All the people I usually competed against were now on my side as we tried to defend our homes.

We could do this. "Okay," I said. "This is just another boss level, folks. A time trial. If we can keep this ogre distracted for . . ." I looked at the Ibis, who flashed her hand three times. "Fifteen minutes. Give me fifteen minutes of your best attacks, and we can win this."

An icon flashed. "Never thought I'd see the day when Yared the Great and the Ibis teamed up, not to mention asking *us* for help." It was Dilla, one of the teens who still played HKO. What we'd call an old-timer. "Excuse me, *Prince* Yared the Great. Don't make it a habit, because this is the only time I'm sticking my neck out for you."

I snorted. "You don't stick your neck out for anything; that's why you're always at the bottom of the leaderboards." The feed erupted in laughter, and I waited for it to settle before speaking again. "Seriously, thank you. Thank you all. If we do this right, our lives will never be the same."

The Bulgu bellowed another bone-rattling challenge, smashing into warehouses on the streets below as it backed up. It looked ready to charge at the underside of the Gebeya again. Why did it have to be so large? Couldn't the Werari have sent a rat-sized creature? That's scary, too.

"All right, everyone," I called. "Here we go. Get its attention and then fall back. Watch the head! We just want to distract it, so do *not* engage. If you get in trouble, ping the *Ezana,* and we'll provide cover. Ready?"

Together, as one, we swept out of the sky. The *Ezana* led the way, the head of a hodgepodge swarm of ships and rust buckets. We flew down, following the curve of the Gebeya around and underneath, until we reached the underside, where a scene of chaos and destruction awaited.

"Is that . . . ?"

"What *is* that thing?"

"We can't —"

"You didn't say . . ."

Voices started talking over the comms all at once at the sight of the Bulgu. The metallic creature shook itself and let out a blast of exhaust. Its giant head lifted and the eyes swiveled around, searching out its target. The chatter on the comms continued to build as shock took hold of our ragtag crew.

I keyed an override and did my best

347

Uncle Moti impersonation, speaking with authority. "Focus! Remember the plan. We just have to distract it long enough for the thrusters to power up."

Even now the giant engines were starting to glow brighter than I'd ever seen, like tiny suns just above our heads. The Bulgu roared again and began to charge. The Ibis sent the *Ezana* forward, approaching the monster at an angle. She nodded at me.

"Now," I said over the comms.

The ships swarmed the bionic beast. We swirled around its head like gnats. At first, I thought it was just going to ignore us, but then one of Haji's drones got too close to the Bulgu's eye and it roared in irritation, swerving aside before continuing to thunder forward. That gave me an idea.

"Haji!" I shouted. "When I say, have your drones target the Bulgu's eyes."

"Won't that make it angry?" the boy asked, pushing his glasses up on his face.

"I hope so. Everyone else, I need you to go to HKO starting formation. Form up around that monster's head and keep your distance!"

"Yared," the Ibis said, looking up at me from her controls. "What are you doing?"

"What my family does best," I said. "Running." I opened the comms. "Ready, Haji? Go!"

Who knew being irritating would one day save the world? I certainly didn't. But there I was, standing on the flight deck of a super-advanced spaceship, leading a group of gamers in a giant match of keep-away-from-the-rampaging-robotic-monster.

And I do mean rampaging.

Haji sent two of his five drones to dive-bomb the Bulgu's right eye, and the beast howled in protest. Every time a drone came near, a metallic lid dropped, briefly blocking the monster's vision. Seconds later, it would open its eye and attempt to resume charging forward. If we could just knock it a bit off course, maybe the Melenik drives would finish powering up.

"Watch it!"

One of the icons on the screen flickered orange. "What happened?" I shouted.

Static filled the comms before Haji's garbled words came through.

". . . got too close. That thing clipped his engines. He's out."

"Safe?"

"Yeah, he's . . . just . . . back."

I hissed in frustration. The Authority Net was wreaking havoc on our comms. We were flying too high. Any higher and —

Another icon flashed orange. Then another. The Bulgu was lashing out as it lumbered forward, swinging its head to clear its vision. I clenched my fists. I hadn't wanted to endanger anyone. "How much time?" I asked the Ibis.

"Five minutes!"

Two more icons flashed orange. "Haji, send the rest of your drones at its eye. Crash them, then you and the others get out of here."

"Are you sure? We can still —"

"No, get to safety. We'll take it from here." As I cut the comms, the Ibis looked at me.

"We will?"

"I hope so. Bring us right in front of that ugly piece of junk at my signal. Wait for it . . . now!"

The last three drones dropped away from Haji's formation, zooming straight at the Bulgu. They slammed into its eye, two of them managing to get past the metal eyelid before it closed. The Bulgu bellowed as it shook its head, clearing the wreckage. When the lid reopened, the *Ezana* hovered right in front of it.

"Lock targeting systems on it," I said.

"We don't have any weapons!"

"It doesn't know that," I said. The Ibis raised her eyebrows, then turned and her hands flew over the controls. A red targeting reticle appeared over the Bulgu's eyes. "Come on," I muttered. This had always been the last resort. I'd hoped to use the confusion of all the ships to lead the beast away, but not if it meant the people I led got hurt. It was up to us. "Take the bait."

The giant red-rimmed eyes narrowed, shifted, then locked onto us. A roar shook the floor beneath us, and the Bulgu lunged forward.

"Here we go!" I shouted. "Reverse

thrusters, we're flying backward."

The Ibis slammed the controls into reverse, and I grabbed the workstation to keep from falling down. If I ever doubted her, the Ibis proved once and for all she was the best pilot I'd ever seen. No, not just the best pilot, the best astrogator. She swerved around buildings and over obstacles as the giant ax head of the Bulgu filled every screen in the *Ezana.* The Gebeya receded into the distance, and I let a small sigh of relief escape my lips. Slowly, the Menelik drives began to reach full power, and bit by bit, the giant, empty market lifted higher in the sky.

Now there was just one more thing to take care of.

"Yared, we can't keep this up for long," the Ibis warned, the strain of concentration making her voice tremble. "We're coming up on Oromo Prime, and the Bulgu is gaining on us."

"Good," I said. We were flying along the main road now. The *Ezana* swerved around abandoned hovercans and parked drones. The ship rattled as we clipped a makeshift barricade. The monster chasing us barreled through it all, crushing anything that got in its way. The Bulgu was charging right at me, its eyes burning with undisguised hatred. "Right back at you," I whispered.

"Yared," the Ibis called.

"Almost there."

"It's right here!"

"Just a bit . . . longer . . ."

The Bulgu lunged forward, the bottom of its ax head nicking one of our thrusters. The *Ezana* spun out of control, and only the Ibis's ace flying saved us from becoming a stain under that beast's foot. But another hit like that and we were done for.

Good thing I wasn't going to let that happen.

The ground disappeared beneath us. We'd reached the lake separating the Oromo Prime woreda from the rest of Addis Prime. The ship sailed backward, and the Bulgu followed. I leaned in. "Get ready to get us out of here," I told the Ibis.

"About time," she muttered.

The Bulgu's metal legs bunched beneath it, and with a mighty spring, it lunged forward. The ax head lifted as it prepared to sever us in half. The Ibis tensed. Besa yowled. I stared, just waiting for the right moment.

The head swung down.

"Now!"

The Ibis slammed the controls forward, whipping the thrusters around and sending the ship into a 180-degree spin. The *Ezana* rolled sideways, slipping past the Bulgu's head with under a meter to spare. The monster's head missed us —

— and sliced into the central Authority tower.

"Go!" I shouted. "Full power!"

We sped off as the sky grew gray. Thousands of Authority drones descended out of the sky, turrets active, spitting a hailstorm of electro-beads at the giant creature attacking Authority property. The Bulgu roared as a stasis field swelled around it, immobilizing it, until it collapsed in a twitching heap.

The monster had fallen.

CHAPTER SEVENTEEN

The Ibis whooped with joy, and Besa leapt into the air, her victory roar filling the flight deck. I let out a shaky breath, the relief sapping the strength from my muscles so that I collapsed into my seat. Everyone still linked on the comms started cheering.

"You did it!"

"Great job!"

"Yared!" Haji shouted. "Is it over? Did we win? Because I have to get these smashed drones back to the repair shop before my sister finds out I took them."

I laughed. "Go ahead. And, Haji?"

"Yeah?"

"Thanks." I leaned forward. "And that goes for everyone. Thank you. Without your help, we wouldn't have been able to do this."

More cheering and hollering filled the flight deck. The *Ezana* swooped back toward the center of town, where the Gebeya was gathering speed as it rose into the sky. With so many drones from the Authority Net focused on the now-captured Bulgu, the floating market had little trouble rising unimpeded through the no-fly zone.

I flicked the info from the screen on my wrist to one of the larger displays in the flight deck. Status updates on the re-engagement process appeared. Everything was green and on track. Axum would be reunited, and then the space station could travel the galaxy again, bringing peace and prosperity to the different worlds it encountered. I sat back and closed my eyes.

"Well done, boy."

The cold voice interrupted the jubilant cheers on the general comms. My breath caught in my throat, and I slowly opened my eyes to see the face of Captain Ascar glaring down at me.

"Who's this?" Haji asked.

"Scatter, Haji!" I shouted. "Run! Code

White!"

Captain Ascar made a gesture with his hand, and all the icons disappeared on the main screen. He was jamming the line, preventing communication between the *Ezana* and any ship that wasn't his own.

"That's better. Just the two of us. Well, I see your little friend and your pet are still alive. No matter. Congratulations are in order! You've managed to subdue the beast. I thought you would fold under the pressure . . . just like your uncle. But don't celebrate too much. You've only delayed the inevitable. When my soldiers land, we will hunt down you and everyone you love. Your family will be ripped apart before you've even had a chance to share a single meal together. Axum will fall, once and for all. Now . . . look up and enjoy the last clear sky you will ever see."

The screen flickered, and Captain Ascar was replaced by a view of the sky. One after another, large, snub-nosed dropships descended through the remnants of the metallic cloud left by the Authority Net. Five, six, seven ships. I pounded the arm of my chair. We'd forgotten about the Werari! No, *I'd* forgotten. That mistake was going to haunt me for however long the Werari allowed us to survive. Some leader. Now everyone was going to suffer.

The dropships rumbled down to the ground, their hatches opening before they'd even completely landed. Trooper after trooper filed out. Rays of sun broke through the dissipating clouds, and the points of the soldiers' shotels shimmered, wickedly sharp and deadly. They lined up four deep in rows that stretched along the central avenue of Addis Prime.

Movement rippled through the center of the line, and a man with a purple demi-cape stepped to the front.

Captain Ascar.

The *Ezana* hovered in place at the other end of the avenue, just above the level of the abandoned buildings. I gripped the armrests of the workstation as I leaned forward to look at the screen. The Ibis's hands were poised over the flight controls. I shook my head. "No. If we leave, the rest of Addis Prime is done for. We need to give them time to escape."

Besa growled next to me, and I nodded.

"Yes. We need to get down there."

The Ibis gawked. "And do what? Talk
them to death? Sacrifice yourself? Don't
be such a fool, Yared. There's nothing you
can do!"

I looked at her. "If it was your family,
what would you do?"

She smacked her teeth and looked
away. After a few seconds, she stood,
flicking the control screen to her wrist
comm. The ship's information appeared
when she rotated her palm. Then she
looked at me. "Fine. Let's go be fools."

"You don't have to —" I started to say,
but she brushed past me and stomped to
the hatch as the Zenaye system piloted
the ship lower to the ground.

"Nope, we're all fools. Come on, you
four-legged fool," she called to Besa. The
lioness padded after her.

"You too?" I asked.

"Mrowr."

"Wow, that hurt."

Outside, the smoke from the demolished businesses clashed with the beautiful afternoon sun. Small fires burned like stars that had fallen to earth, and the metallic odors singed my nostrils. My eyes pricked with tears as the breeze carried dust into my eyes. I looked up. Bright blue patches of sky gleamed through the glittering silver ribbons of the remaining Authority Net. It was like the setting of a fever dream, one I might not wake up from.

The *Ezana* hovered above us. Dirt crunched under my boots, and piles of rubble lay everywhere. A pipe with jagged pieces of a diranium panel at the end protruded from one pile. I picked it up and hefted it.

"If we're going to lose," I said, "we'll make the Werari earn every bit of space they defile."

Besa roared and shook her ridge of spikes loose. Her tail lashed left and right as she roared again and again. The Ibis tapped a command on her wrist, and the *Ezana*'s thrusters fired in response. "They won't get the ship," she promised. "Not in the way they want, anyway." She picked up a long pole with a spear-like tip and twirled it. It looked like I wasn't the only one ready to go down fighting. I grinned, then started walking toward the Werari.

"Don't be silly, boy!" Captain Ascar yelled as we approached the wall of white-armored soldiers. "Surrender. No one has to lose their life. Come with us, and I promise everything will be okay."

"That's where you're wrong," I shouted. "The day we surrender is the day nothing will be okay. The day we surrender is the day our lives have already been lost. So no. I think we'll fight. One more time."

I looked at the Ibis. "One more time," I said again, softly.

She nodded as Besa nuzzled my hand. "We're with you."

I tried to smile, but my vision sparkled as tears piled on my lashes. Not trusting myself to speak, I spun without another word and sprinted forward. I heard the Ibis's footsteps close behind me. Besa's snarl turned into a full-throated roar that merged with the sound of the *Ezana*'s engines as the Axumite ship blasted forward.

A hundred meters to go. Captain Ascar's face twisted with hatred. He raised his arm.

Fifty meters. The Werari stepped forward.

Twenty meters. I could see their faces. Or maybe I imagined them. The sun winked off their shotels, like stars on earth.

Ten meters. More stars blinked into existence in the sky above. Bright orange, trailing smoke behind them as they fell. So many . . . they descended like a meteor shower.

Wait.

"Proud of you, my lion," came a familiar voice.

Besa roared, and I skidded to a stop only a few meters from the Werari. The troopers had turned in confusion and disarray. They shouted orders as they tried to reset against this new threat.

"What's happening?" the Ibis asked.

"I'm not sure," I said, looking around in awe.

Exo after exo landed, shaking the

ground with each impact. Most had black-and-gold armor plating, and the insignia of a roaring lion with a bloodred mane was etched on their shoulders. Some had shotels drawn, others had warbows or lightspears. They stood a full meter higher than the Werari. Even though the troopers outnumbered these newcomers, they were no match.

Captain Ascar let out a snarl and lunged forward, gloved fingers clawing at my neck. I yelped and tried to duck backward, but my feet got tangled with Besa's tail and I stumbled. Just as the captain's hand grazed me, an armored gauntlet came out of nowhere and seized it.

"Ascar."

Both Captain Ascar and I looked up as a huge silver-and-gold exo stepped between us. The armored fighter lifted the leader of the Werari up by his wrist, until he dangled in midair. The captain struggled, but he was no match for the exo. With a flick of a diranium wrist, my savior sent Captain Ascar flying through the air. He landed in a heap, skidding along the ground until he came to a stop at the feet of a second wave of exos. He started to rise, then froze when the tip of a shotel landed on his shoulder.

"Please, try to get up," said the pilot of the silver-and-gold exo. "Make that mistake, I am begging you."

Captain Ascar spat out a clod of dirt, then collapsed back to the ground.

A few of the Werari tried to put up fights, but after a familiar beat-up exo backhanded a soldier through a collapsed office building — then asked if anyone wanted coffee — the rest surrendered. I saw Captain Ascar face-down on the ground, a warbow inches away from his face, when a shadow fell over me.

The gold-and-silver exo with shoulder-mounted thrusters landed heavily on the ground. It towered over the Ibis and me. The faceshield slid up, and I couldn't help it. The widest grin split my face.

"Is that . . . ?" the Ibis began to ask, but I didn't stay to listen. I leapt forward and hugged the man who'd always had my back.

"That is General Moti Berihun and his famed Burning Legion." I looked at the man who'd risked his life, his reputation, and his nation to protect me. Who'd raised me. Sometimes family isn't just those people related to you by blood; it's the ones we have chosen to love. "That . . . is my uncle Moti."

Uncle Moti looked at me and winked, then waved his hands at the Werari. "Why don't I take it from here?" he said.

The Gebeya soared upward. A lot of the structure had fallen way — some parts heavily damaged from the Bulgu's attacks, others unable to survive the high-speed exit from the atmosphere. That left the central core of the structure, along with the three working Menelik drives. Together, they formed a rough polyhedral shape and a bright bluish-white plume trailing behind it.

"Beautiful, isn't it?" Uncle Moti stood at my side on the flight deck of the *Ezana*. Besa rested on her haunches between us, and the Ibis stood to my right. Kamali leaned against a workstation on the other side of Uncle Moti, and the five of us watched the holo-display floating in midair. In it, the great obelisk of Axum spun slowly as it awaited the return of its drive system. I drank that image in. All this time, while participating in HKO, I'd never dreamed the actual obelisk that inspired it could be so beautiful. And soon it would be whole. Bright, thin red lines representing vectors and trajectories constantly updated as a clock timer counted down to the moment when the giant space station reengaged.

"Five hours," I said out loud.

A speaker crackled, and a woman's voice filled the flight deck. "Don't sound so nervous, young prince," said Captain Leyu. The Meshenitai leader had contacted us soon after all the Werari were rounded up. Apparently the Guardians had helped to turn the tide against the few Werari remaining on Axum. The important thing was that my mother and father — the Emperor and Empress — were okay. But if we were going to have any hope of rebuilding the damage caused by the decade of Werari meddling, as well the battles on Addis Prime, Axum needed the power of the Menelik drives.

And the key to unlocking them lay within me. The future of Axum, Addis

366

Prime, and the people who called both home relied on me.

So yeah . . . I think a little nervousness was called for.

"Nope, totally not nervous," I lied.

"Relax, my son." Everyone straightened up when the voice of the Empress came through the display. The screen minimized, and my mother's face took its place. She smiled at me, then nodded at Uncle Moti. "The general has informed me that everything is in order."

Uncle Moti bowed. "It is, my queen."

"And the monster?"

"Subdued and watched constantly until the containment field arrives."

The Bulgu had been hauled out of the reservoir by a collection of construction drones, then flown under guard to one of the old factories in the highlands. Uncle Moti had felt it was better to get the creature out of sight as quickly as possible, in order to squash any panic that might arise.

The Empress nodded. "It will take time to heal from its destruction, and from the Werari. But with the capabilities of

Axum restored, we will be able to assist."

"Are they beaten, Your Highness, Empress, ma'am?" the Ibis asked. "The Werari, I mean."

The screen rippled, and then another face joined my mother's side. The Emperor. My father. His stern expression surveyed the flight deck, then his gaze landed on me. He smiled, briefly, before turning to the Ibis.

"Not completely, no. If only that were the case. I'm afraid they will retreat and lick their wounds. But we will be watching for their return, and won't stand idly by. The Axumite Empire may have lost much during our isolation, but we will recover. We must recover."

The Empress turned to me, a proud expression on her face. "Enough of that, dear. Now isn't the time for the future. It's for the present. We have much to do, and the first thing is for me to hug my son again."

"I wouldn't dream of delaying that," my father said, a smile hovering on his lips.

"So, my heart, my lion, my prince, and

my son . . . are you ready?" My mother held out her arms, and even though it was a virtual display, my chest ached with the joy the gesture contained.

"I am," I said. Uncle Moti's palm dropped to my shoulder, and I felt the Ibis take my hand. "I'm so ready."

"We are, too, my dear. It's time for you to come home."

Audio Transcript File No. 2137.023

Location: Axum Capital, Space Station Module Harar

Time: 14:30

Subject: Prince Yared I, Crown Prince of Axum

Me: So there you have it. One epic story of how an awesome kid got even more awesome. Awesomer? The awesomest.

[loud roar off camera]

Me: But it's true!

[indistinct yowl]

Me: Fine, you don't have to be so rude. Anyway, so maybe that's not exactly what the story is about. Maybe it's about how we love family, find family, and maybe even choose family.

Me: Oh yeah, I snagged this handy surveillance drone from the Imperial Security office. They won't need it. Besides, do you know how cool it would be to rig up an HKO video drone? I could stream all my matches!

[exasperated growl]

Me: Well, you go watch *her* matches, then! Jeez. Speaking of, you'll be happy to know the Ibis's family is safe. Her parents and siblings can travel to and from the orbitals without fear of being harassed by the Authority. Which is good, because the Ibis really needs more practice with that flying death trap of hers. Seriously. You're only as good as your rival, they say.

[annoyed yowl]

Me: I don't know who they is, they just say it!

[low growl]

Me: Just whose Guardian are you? Traitor. Anyway, they rescheduled HKO for a later date. I'm hoping I'm back before then so I can take part. Haji and the Toe Twins promised to hold my spot. Just because I'm a prince doesn't mean I don't have other crowns to defend. The Ibis will be there, too, I suppose.

Me: Oh! And guess who's paid up on all their tuition? That's right. Suddenly, Addis Prime Primary is "delighted" that I'm a student there and would be "thrilled" if I returned next year. SMH. But Mrs. Marjani did send me a screen loaded with all the homework for the rest of the semester so I wouldn't fall behind. I mean, she's cool and all, but wow . . . Wowwwww.

Zenaye System: Ten minutes until reengagement.

Me: That's my cue! We're off to find one of the ring sections and reconnect it to Axum. I'm pretty excited about it. My first trip to a different star system. Mom says we have to be careful, because apparently the ring section was left in a troublesome quadrant. Some old one-star system. She said there was a planet there that was pretty cool in the past, and a galactic council used to be based there — basically a bunch of grown-ups telling each other what to do. Yeah, pretty boring, right? But if Axum is going to rebuild itself, it's going to need all the help it can get. So, off we go! Anyway, if you get this message, come find me. I'm always looking for new friends. This is Prince Yared I of Axum, signing off.

Me: Oh yeah, before I forget, the planet's called Earth. See you there?

AFTERWORD BY PRINCE JOEL MAKONNEN

Dear Reader,

Thank you for joining us on this epic trek through the *Last Gate of the Emperor.*

Just like our protagonist, Yared Heywat, who's on a journey to discover who he really is, I had a similar path in my life. Of course, Yared goes on a grand adventure with his bionic lioness, Besa, to trace back his roots to the Axumite Empire and fight off an invading force! But even though this book is set in a fantastical, futuristic Ethiopia, the world in *Last Gate* is very much inspired by real places and people.

Growing up, I had no idea of the magnitude of my ancestry. I spent my childhood in Geneva, Switzerland, and attended boarding school in the neighboring French Alps. It was always snow-

375

ing and cold! Late nights, way after the cooking staff had given us our supper, a few roommates and I would sneak back into the kitchens to "borrow" some cheese plates. Then we would gather around in the main TV room, wrapped in our blankets, and have us a great cheese banquet. It would warm our bellies and our spirits in the middle of the long Savoyard winters. One time, I remember sharing with the group that I was the great-grandson of Haile Selassie, the late Ethiopian emperor. One of the boys said, "Yeah right, and my father is Bill Clinton!" This kid was not the US president's son, nor did he even look related to the Clintons; he was from Côte d'Ivoire, a country in West Africa. :-)

So, I became reluctant to share this information, because people either didn't believe me, or if they did, they'd ask me so many questions, like "Where is your palace?" "How many butlers do you have?" I'd think, "Yeah, where is all that?!" My family told me very little about our past and preferred keeping a low profile. After all, a communist revolution shook our nation and the entire royal family was scattered. My parents; my older brother, Yoki; and I were living in exile in Europe. So, it was only over years of wondering and inquiring, and the "Uncle Motis" in *my* life telling me bits and pieces, that I finally put it all together. And what I discovered was a revelation. I was a descendant of the "Solomonic Dynasty," the oldest monarchy in the world. And just like our young hero, Yared, my true story gave me so much power. Here's a glimpse into that history, and the real people and regions that inspired our book.

It all started about . . . three thousand years ago! The Queen of Sheba heard about King Solomon of Israel's great wisdom and decided to pay him a visit at his palace in Jerusalem. It's said they took a great liking to each other and spent a night together. Later, the queen bore a son from King Solomon and she named him Menelik. Emperor Menelik I thus founded the Solomonic Dynasty, which ruled Ethiopia for the next three millennia. His empire was the precursor to what later would become known as the Kingdom of Axum. The most prominent Axumite kings were King Ezana and King Kaleb. In the fourth century AD, King Ezana was the first monarch of the line to convert the kingdom to Christianity. Later came King Kaleb, who is most famous for having fought off the Arabian armies of the Himyarite king who sought to invade Axum. This victory earned him the title of Saint Elesbaan, Defender of the Christian Faith, from religious leaders in Rome and Greece. The end of King Kaleb's life is shrouded in mystery, however, as he is said to have abdicated his throne and retreated to a monastery. No one knows where he was buried. The famous obelisks of Axum are markers of a king's burial place; therefore, the Hunt for Kaleb's Obelisk continues!

Centuries later, Emperor Haile Selassie I would become the 225th and last monarch of the ancient Solomonic line. Like his predecessors, he retained the title of "King of Kings," which refers to the fact that Ethiopia was made up of several regions, each led by a different king. Thus, the emperor was the king of all kings, serving as a unifying figure under whom to rally and fight off would-be invaders. Throughout history, Ethiopia is well known for remaining independent and never being colonized.

I hope this story will have sparked your curiosity to learn even more about Ethiopia as one of the great civilizations of the world. And I also hope that as you read *Last Gate,* you'll be inspired to discover your own history, no matter who you are or where you're from. I'm sure you'll find some surprises, some magic, and that — like Yared — you'll discover there's nothing more powerful than embracing your true self.

ACKNOWLEDGMENTS

Kwame

A story that spans the galaxy has to begin somewhere. I have to give a special thanks to my wife, my Axum, my world. I don't get to write stories without her in my life.

To Joel, thank you for riding with me. This journey is only just beginning, and the stars are in the future.

To the incredible teams at Scholastic and Cake Literary, thank you for the drive and momentum behind the book, and for getting this story in front of the readers who deserve to see themselves throughout the universe.

And to the Yareds of the world who are searching for their own story, I see you.

Joel

This book makes my heart swell with pride when I see how far we've come in making it a reality, with an entire village behind it. Thank you to everyone who made me and this book possible.

Thank you to all those who came before me, my ancestors, forebearers, kings and queens from a millenary dynasty, whose history lives through me and my family, who have given me my identity, inspiration, strength, and pride, and whose noble and powerful legacy I've inherited. I stand on the shoulders of all these giants. To Ethiopia, my home country, and to all her people.

A gigantic thank-you to my amazing friend Dhonielle Clayton, whose drive for this project launched us on a journey to bring a young African boy hero to the world of children's literature. This book has simultaneously satisfied some of our most burning desires — mine, of telling my family and country's proud history in an accessible way for younger readers, and hers, of expressing the vision of a rich, gilded Ethiopia that would shine in the imagination of young minds everywhere. I am forever grateful; thank you.

A massive thank-you to my incredible coauthor, le grand Kwame Mbalia. We met, we instantly clicked, and the rest is history, as they say. A pure match made in Axumite heaven. You are such a talented writer, you care for and respect this history just as much as I do, and you brought this story to life in such a fun and adventurous way. You are simply the best collaborator I could have asked for. A heartfelt thank-you, my brother.

To my loving wife, Ariana, who is always by my side bringing the best out of me and making me want to be better each day.

To my dear mother, Adey, who made me who I am. She is the sweetest mother and person I know in the whole world. Thank you for always believing in me and giving me unconditional love. You mean the universe to me.

To my dearest auntie Saba, who has been my biggest cheerleader since I was a little boy and always has the right words to encourage me.

To my dear grandmother Martha, who left us this year when God called her back home so that she may be an angel and watch over us. You remain forever in my heart and I know this story would make you so proud. And to my grandfather "Papiye," a true guardian of Ethiopian history and culture.

To all my family and loved ones, my late father, Prince David, my grandmother Princess Sara, and all our other dearest departed ones, recently or a dynasty ago.

Thank you to Ozi Menakaya and Cindy Uh at CAA, and my super attorney Jesseca Salky.

To Cake Literary, to Joanna and the New Leaf team, and all others who worked to support the making of *Last Gate.*

A very special thanks to David Levithan and Zachary Clark at Scholastic for your immense belief and infectious enthusiasm for Yared's story — history will remember you as the very first *Last Gate* fans — and the whole Scholastic team for your amazing support and excitement from the start.

To the superb illustrator Setor Fiadzigbey, creator of a fantastic cover for the ages, thank you.

And thank you to the readers for joining us on this epic journey. Venture on to Axum!

ABOUT THE AUTHORS

Kwame Mbalia is a husband, a father, a writer, a *New York Times* bestselling author, and a former pharmaceutical metrologist, in that order. He is the author of *Tristan Strong Punches a Hole in the Sky,* a Coretta Scott King Honor book. He lives with his family in North Carolina. Visit him online at Kwame mbalia.com.

Prince Joel Makonnen is the great-grandson of His Imperial Majesty Emperor Haile Selassie I, the last emperor of Ethiopia. He is an attorney and the cofounder of Old World/New World, a media and entertainment company focused on telling powerful African stories that inspire global audiences through film, TV, and books. He lives with his wife, Ariana, in Los Angeles. Visit him online at princeyoel.com.